STAR RIDERS

STAR RIDERS

*Josephine
Pullein-Thompson*

*Allen Junior
Fiction*

STAR RIDERS was first published as STAR-RIDERS OF THE MOOR
by Hodder and Stoughton in 1976
Revised Allen Junior Fiction edition 1990
Text © Josephine Pullein-Thompson
Illustrations © J A Allen 1990

British Library Cataloguing in Publication Data
Pullein-Thompson, Josephine
    Star riders. —Rev. ed.
    I. Title   II. Pullein-Thompson, Josephine. Star-riders of
    the moor.
    I. Title
    823.914 [J]

    ISBN 0-85131-519-4

ONE

For all the time we'd lived in St. Dinas, which was three-quarters of my life, there had only been three horsey families in the neighbourhood. The Burnetts — that's us, me, Frances, and my younger sister Louisa. The Mitchells, William and Carolyn and the Jacksons, Heather, Mick and Tracy. So, when my father walked in on this evening at the beginning of the Easter holidays and announced the arrival of two new families with four children who rode, Louisa and I were delighted.

'Boys or girls?' 'How old are they?' 'Have they got ponies?' Ignoring our questions Daddy poured himself a drink and collapsed into a chair with a groan. Mummy asked tactfully about the measles epidemic raging in Baybourne and wearing out all the local doctors of whom Daddy is one. Then we got him back to the point.

'Well the most important child is called Jane Shaw. She and her mother have come to live at Chapel Cottages. There seems to have been a divorce, anyway there's no father in evidence, and Mrs. Shaw decided to come here because she had happy memories of childhood holidays in Tolbay. She's fixed herself up with a secretarial job in Baybourne and the wretched Jane will be on her own all day. I said you'd look after her.'

'But Daddy, supposing she's ghastly; really *Ugh*?' I protested indignantly. 'You oughtn't to have landed us with her just like that.'

Daddy's rather long face put on its public-spirited-look, 'She's thirteen, she rides, she looks a perfectly normal girl and we can't leave a child of that age alone in a strange village, so, ghastly or not, you'll have to look after her until she finds her feet.'

'And what about the other family?' asked Louisa.

'Oh, they don't need any help from us,' said Daddy as though that made them less interesting. 'Father's Stewart Hamilton, you've seen him on the box, large, blond bloke. He did a programme on his trek through the foothills of Nepal and another one, on Thailand was it? Or the border of Burma? Anyway, he's bought Penhydrock and moved his wife and three sons in just as it is. He says they've had enough of London and the Home Counties, they're going to live the simple life and grow their own vegetables.'

'The damp and draughty life,' said Mummy. 'There are great holes in the roof and the whole place is rotting away.'

'How old are they?' I asked.

'A bit younger than me.'

'No, not the parents, the boys.'

'Two of them look about your age and then there's a younger one; they've a pony apiece.'

Mummy began to ask questions about the two

mothers and to wonder what the Hamiltons would do with Penhydrock, which was once a lovely house but had been allowed to go to rack and ruin by two old sisters who'd lived there for years and years and finally died in their nineties. Then she began to wonder what poor Mrs. Shaw would do with number three Chapel Cottages, one of a tall, grim terrace of grey stone cottages and full, according to Mummy, of horrid little box-shaped rooms. Daddy picked up the paper and, realising we would learn no more, Louisa and I went back to the kitchen to finish our tack-cleaning. I was pleased about the Hamiltons, two more boys would even things up a bit, and though I like William he always behaves in a very elder-brotherly way and crushes us all with his superior knowledge. Mick's an even nicer person, brilliant at making jumps, mending tack, giving colic drenches, but he never says very much; he lets Heather do all the talking.

As ponies make conversation so much easier, you can always admire them or even give them a pat when you run out of things to say, so we decided to take ours with us when we went next day to call on Jane. We groomed them long and energetically: brushing out great lumps of moulting hair and made them look as smart as unclipped ponies can in April. In the summer Redwing is very elegant; gazelle-like is how I'd describe her. She's a thirteen-three red roan mare with black points, very slender and well-bred-looking with a finely cut head and huge eyes, but since she had a pony mother and was bred and brought up on the moor, she's very clever and sure-footed.

Louisa's Spider, a compact little brown pony, has a

star which looks as though the paint ran while it was still wet and he obviously got his name from its spidery drips. He's one of those lovely easy ponies, obliging and sensible and a very reliable jumper up to his limit which is three-foot-three. He only has one fault; over-eating in summer, and that does make terrible problems.

Rosebank, our house, was built by a Victorian doctor. It stands in a sheltered coomb at the south end of the village and looks away from the moor, over Penhydrock and Ruveland, towards Tolbay. The main part of St. Dinas, the church, the chapel, the post office and the row of cottages, might be in another world though they are only a quarter of a mile away, they stand on the highest part of the road with the moor all round them. They *do* have beautiful views in the summer, but in the winter the moor can look very bleak and the buildings standing in a long grey row seem very much at the mercy of gales and storms. Then driving rain and blizzards sweep relentlessly over the moor and the wind howls hungrily, rattling doors and windows as though trying to break in. Most people who have come to live at Chapel Cottages moved out after their first winter, except for two or three of the oldest in-habitants of St. Dinas who remember sterner days, before electricity and bathrooms and television, and anyway have grown so deaf that they no longer hear the wind's frustrated howls.

As we rode towards number three we started a slight argument about who should knock on the door. I said it was Louisa's turn to do something embarrassing as I had answered our door to the Vicar and he'd gone on and on about the fête, one day when Mummy was out.

Louisa said that I was older and so ought to be less embarrassed and generally better at managing life than she was; this is one of our parents' arguments for making me do things Louisa won't. I had begun to point out all the things I had had to do at nine which she still wouldn't do at twelve, when the door of number three opened and a slim woman appeared, dressed in a paint-spattered sweater and trousers with a red-spotted handkerchief tied over her hair and wearing glasses.

She said 'Hullo' and I asked if she was Mrs. Shaw and explained that we were the Burnetts and had come to see Jane. Mrs. Shaw gave eager cries and Jane came thundering down the uncarpeted stairs. She was large for thirteen with fuzzy dark hair; like her mother she wore glasses and was spattered with paint. I didn't feel very enthusiastic about her at first sight, but when, on seeing the ponies, she gave a shriek of delight, threw down her paint brush and rushed out to pat them, I decided that she might be better than she looked.

As Jane asked Louisa the names, ages and habits of the ponies I dismounted and discussed with Mrs. Shaw the scenery and the best way to get to Tolbay and the awfulness of living in a London suburb. Then as Jane seemed so terribly horsey. I asked if she would like to try Redwing. She mounted in a flash and began to let my stirrups down while her mother rushed upstairs to find her crash cap. She looked a bit top heavy on Redwing who really isn't up to weight. William once said that she was a thoroughbred weed with both forelegs coming out of the same hole, but that was partly because she was faster than his pony and he didn't like it. I wondered whether he would leave us all trailing behind now that he had a horse. Louisa and Jane set off up the road and vanished from sight. I stifled my anxieties and accepted Mrs. Shaw's offer of elevenses.

We went into the kitchen, which, she said, was the only habitable room in the cottage and made coffee and ate chocolate biscuits. At first she made boring remarks about Daddy being a super doctor and Louisa looking just like him, but then she began to talk about buying Jane a pony and became quite sensible. I told her about the Jacksons. How Heather, Mick and Tracy were our friends and how Mr. Jackson had a small farm with a lot of grazing rights on the moor and dealt in ponies and ran trekking holidays in the summer. 'If you want an ordinary pony for riding over the moor you can't do better than the Jacksons,' I explained. 'But if you're looking for something grander — a showjumper or —'

'No, no, we can't possibly afford anything grand,' she interrupted me quickly. 'That was the trouble at Headslow, half the children had thousand-pound showjumpers or eventers. Even the gymkhana ponies seemed to be four or five hundred; we just felt that we couldn't compete. But here, with all this lovely country to ride over you must be able to have fun with an ordinary pony, surely?'

'Yes, we do. Some people ride in shows, but it's always such miles to get to them, we use our ponies mostly for transport; we're always taking messages or looking for lost sheep or checking up on ponies that are due to foal.'

Mrs. Shaw became so eager about the prospect of

seeing Mr. Jackson that in the end I agreed to take her, and we drawing-pinned a large notice to the front door.

'Gone to Black Tor Farm to see about a pony. Follow at once,' and both signed it.

We passed the rest of Chapel Cottages; the post office set back from the road behind a little fence, soap powders and sweets dimly displayed in its old-fashioned paned window; the church, sharply spired among its hump-backed yews and tumbling tombs. Then, where the road turned downhill, the Jacksons' farm began and we turned left up the stone walled lane between the tiny fields that someone, years and years ago, had coaxed out of the moor. We were half-way along the lane with the grey stone farm buildings in sight and Black Tor, a small, solitary hill topped by a great black rock dominating the moor behind, when we heard hoofs and Louisa and Jane came trotting in pursuit.

Jane said, 'Oh she's lovely; absolutely gorgeous!' and flung herself off Redwing, shrieking, 'No!' in a very determined manner when I suggested that she should ride on to the farm. So Louisa and I decided to trot ahead to warn the Jacksons of prospective buyers and start the long and complicated process of finding suitable ponies.

The sign *Black Tor Trekking Centre* blown down by the winter winds still leaned drunkenly against the ancient hay-rake, with its curved prongs and broken shafts that had stood abandoned for years among the nettles by the gate. The stone barns and byres straggled round the low stone farm-house making it difficult to tell where buildings ended and house began.

Shouting, 'Heather, Mick, Tracy,' we rode up to the back door. A row of disconsolate, shivering dogs and three cross-looking cats waiting outside, told us that Mrs. Jackson was in a bad mood. But still, this was business. I put my head nervously round the door and asked, 'Is Mr. Jackson about? We've got Mrs. Shaw here and she wants to buy a pony.'

'I don't know and I don't care,' began Mrs. Jackson, with an angry clatter of baking tins and then, as the end of my sentence sank in, 'Wants to buy a pony, does she? Well, they're all out on the moor catching up the ponies he promised the London family, that bought a cottage at Pennecford. They booked special ones and he woke up this morning and remembered they were all turned out.' She banged a pastry hat angrily on a pie dish.

I said, 'O.K. we'll go and look for them.' I exchanged a conspiratorial look with the dogs who had been slinking in between my legs and were now sitting in a grateful row with their backs against the Rayburn cooker, and went back to Louisa and the ponies. When we had shouted our intentions to the Shaws and told them to look around the ponies in the yard, for the stable and the barn and every little sheep pen was always stuffed with ponies at the Jackson's, we whirled away across a little field, over a stone wall into the next field and out over another wall to the moor. We knew the path out across West Moor well. It was very narrow and wound and twisted to avoid boulders and boggy patches and stony ground, but we left the steering to the ponies who were both experts and enjoyed wild gallops over the moor just as much as we did. I was in the lead because Redwing is faster than Spider and presently Louisa called, 'Spider wants a breather.' Then, as I slowed down, she called again, 'There's Mick, over by the plantation.'

I looked across to Barley Bog on which, long ago, a square black plantation of firs had been planted to drain the bog and save the yearly toll of cows, sheep and ponies which it had sucked into its slimy depths, and saw Mick on grey Silver Sand vanishing round the corner. We turned into the heather, found a path going in the right direction and set off after Mick. As we rounded the plantation we found the Jacksons all converging on a group of trotting, snorting ponies. We joined the half circle and helped to edge the ponies up to the plantation fence. At first they tried to break out, darting and dodging with bright eyes and flowing manes and tails, but we calmed them down with soothing cries and our slow approach. Suddenly they gave in, you could tell at once; the challenge went out of their eyes, their heads drooped, they became bored and submissive. Mick dismounted, gave them all handfuls of nuts, slipped head-collars on the ponies which were wanted. I rode over to Mr. Jackson and told him about the waiting Shaws.

'Want to buy a pony,' he repeated, his eyes brightening. 'I suppose Pirate wouldn't suit them?'

'No, he's far too small.' That was much easier than pointing out that Pirate was such a little beast that no one could possibly want to buy him.

Mr. Jackson scratched his wiry, grey-sprinkled, black hair thoughtfully. 'Well this lot from London want Mousie and Gipsy for the parents and Poppy and Tinker for the kids, so they're promised for the week. There's Trudy ...'

Louisa had told Heather about Jane and she came cantering up and said, 'Come on Dad, Mrs. Shaw's waiting.' She tossed one of the ponies' ropes to me. Mr. Jackson, who is always shocking us by his awful riding, gave his pony a jerk in the mouth and a kick with his gum-booted heels and we all set off as fast as we could go with led ponies on the narrow paths.

Tracy was having trouble with Pirate as usual. He is a small-eyed, mean-natured little black pony of about twelve hands. He was stopping dead to graze whenever he saw a patch of spring grass and then tearing after the rest of us at a breakneck speed. Tracy, pale and rather feeble with a meek little voice and dead straight, shoulder length fair hair, isn't a bit like the other Jacksons. Heather has fair hair but it's golden and curly and she's noisy, tough and determined. Mick's quiet, but he's very calm and competent and his hair is a sort of hay colour and is cut in a thick thatch. They always have rather smart hairstyles because Dawn, the eldest sister, was a hairdresser before she married and every time she comes to see them she drags them off their ponies and gets to work.

As I came up to the wall into the first field Mr. Jackson was waiting to shout threats at my led pony in case it tried to refuse, but it didn't and we whizzed on over the next wall and into the yard. The Shaws looked rather bewildered at the arrival of so many ponies, but I introduced them to the Jacksons and explained again that they wanted a sensible pony of fourteen-two, not too expensive.

Mr. Jackson sent Tracy to fetch Trudy, bemoaned the fact that Gipsy and Mousie were promised for a week and wondered whether Crackers would do. Heather said that he was big enough but not really sensible. In the end Jane tried six ponies. Trudy who is a vast dun, all round and upholstered like a sofa, and very slow; Crackers, a fiery black who ran away round the field with her and would have jumped the yard gate only we all waved our arms and yelled; Mousie and Gipsy whom she couldn't have; Silver Sand, who stargazes slightly, with Mick, but became steadily worse with her; and finally Misty, the very dirty, sweaty, long-ungroomed grey that Mr. Jackson had been riding. Misty suited her best so, as we were all weak with hunger and it was long past lunchtime, it was hastily agreed that she should hire Misty for a week and see how things went. Then the question of a field arose. Everyone thought that Mrs. Jackson's mother would let her little paddock across the stream from ours but meanwhile the only place seemed the garden of number three. As Mrs. Shaw said there was nothing to eat there, it was totally overgrown with weeds and brambles, but it had a stout wall round it and if they fed Misty as though she were stabled she would be quite comfortable until the ground got cut up and muddy.

Louisa and I offered to lend hay and oats until Mr. Jackson could deliver and we also volunteered to help look for yew seedlings, that might have blown in from the churchyard, and other poisonous plants.

I offered Mrs. Shaw Redwing for the homeward journey, but she said that she hadn't ridden for donkeys years and was quite happy to walk, so Jane, Louisa and I went on ahead to organise Misty's lunch. We agreed that she should be kept tied up until we'd all eaten ours and carried out the inspection of the garden.

Mummy was slightly annoyed that we were so late. She said that our lunches would be like leather and that she didn't mind what time we came home if only we would *say*. We explained about the Shaws' pony-buying and pointed out that Daddy had said we were to look after Jane. Then, hearing that I had actually been inside number three, Mummy cheered up and demanded a full description.

TWO

Louisa and I were quarrelling when Jane came round next morning. Daddy had announced at breakfast that old Mrs. Hinds was down with bronchitis again, her son had telephoned the surgery on his way to work, and he wanted to get some antibiotic down her as soon as possible. Mrs. Cole would have it ready by ten and we were to take it over to St. Crissy.

It was Mummy's day for handicapped children and we'd planned to go for a long ride, up Northmoor to Menacoell which is my favourite place. Now we were being sent in almost the opposite direction. I was cross. I grumbled as I groomed Redwing and Louisa said I was selfish. She really is more like Daddy than I am; as well as his long face she has his serious nature and she means to be a doctor. Sometimes I think that they both actually *prefer* giving up things to having them; I'm quite the other way round.

Anyway, hearing hoofs we stopped quarrelling and hurried out of our Victorian stable, built by the Victorian doctor, to see who had come. Misty was a dazzling white and almost unrecognisable. Her mane and tail

were so exquisitely brushed out that she looked ready
to win a Mountain and Moorland Class at any minute.
Jane, pleased with our amazement, said she'd been up
since six and I could believe she worked every minute
of that time, for I don't think Misty had ever had more
than ten minutes with a dandy brush in her life before.
She'd cleaned the tack too and it was now unbelievably
supple and shiny for Jackson trekking tack. When we'd
admired Misty from every angle Jane said that she'd
come to ask if we were going riding and whether she
could come with us. We explained about Mrs. Hinds
and our errand and said that she could certainly come if
she liked.

The surgery, or Health Centre, as it has been grandly
renamed since they built on to it, is in Ruveland, the
next tiny village on the narrow winding road to Tolbay.
We rode between high, primrose covered banks; we
passed Penhydrock, the sagging, moss-encrusted gate
stood open as usual, the drive plunged down into a
tunnel of evergreens, trees and shrubs which, un-
pruned for years, had grown into a leafy jungle that
entirely hid the house from the road. Louisa and I
looked and listened hopefully for signs of the Hamiltons,
we were longing to see them, but Jane was rather
dampening. She said having a famous father would
have made them very stuck up and she was sure they
had thousand-pound ponies.

Mrs. Cole had two packets of medicine waiting for
us. One was a bottle of cough mixture and she sternly
forbade us to jump a single wall before we'd delivered
it. She's never forgiven me for smashing one of her

horrid brews when I fell off and landed on a boulder, an accident from which my poor anorak never recovered.

A few yards from the Health Centre the moor ends officially, with a cattle grid set in the road and a gate beside it for riders and herds of cows and flocks of sheep. But we turned right, up a lane that would take us back to the moor. We passed a pair of deserted cottages with grass growing from their roofs. There are a lot of these on the moor because few people want to live in wild spots without electricity and piped water and telephones. Some have been restored to let as holiday cottages, but most just stand broken and forlorn until they subside back into heaps of stones.

We came out on the moor near Old Dog, a long hill with a craggy mound at one end. It is supposed to look like a dog lying down and it does vaguely if you look at it from the Barley Bog side, but not from any other angle. We rode soberly to preserve the cough mixture and we were past Old Dog and heading for the ruined tower that stands above St. Crissy when we saw three riders approaching; they weren't Jacksons and they didn't look like the Londoners from Pennecford. They were strangers on strange ponies. As we drew nearer I saw that they were all boys and realised that they might be the Hamiltons. The one on the tallest pony kept stopping to consult a map and what looked like one of those large, complicated compasses in a leather case. Their voices carried on the clear, quiet air of the empty moor and we could hear the smallest one pleading with his brother, 'Do ask those girls, Felix, I'm sure they know.' Then the middle one said something and Felix threw the map at him and shouted, 'Well, if you're so brilliant you do it.'

Louisa and I looked at each other, wondering whether to ride straight on, which would mean a confrontation, or to take some aimless little sheep path that would allow us to pass at a distance. I decided to be brave. I screwed up my courage firmly. One boy would have been quite easy, but three was rather a collection to face. As we got near I said, 'Hullo,' and they said 'Hullo' back and got off the path to let us pass. I stopped and asked, 'Are you the new people at Penhydrock?'

'Yes, that's right.' 'That's us.' The two larger boys answered together, while the smaller one looked pleased, as though he felt more at home in this wild land now that he had been heard of. I explained who we were and about our errand to St. Crissy. They introduced themselves as Felix, Toby and Huw. Then Toby asked, 'You're *going* to St. Crissy?'

'Yes, it's over there, just below the ruined tower; that's Tolkenny Castle.' I pointed. 'It's haunted; the ponies hate going there.'

'Oh, Spider doesn't mind that much,' Louisa protested. 'He's more secure than Redwing.' I was about to point out that most of the Great are tiresomely neurotic when Toby turned to Felix. 'I told you you'd got the map upside down, you great fool. You said St. Crissy was over there.' He pointed towards home. 'Now we've spent hours riding in the wrong direction and it's too late to see the castle; we've wasted the whole morning thanks to you.'

Felix's face had turned scarlet, but I could see that he didn't want to quarrel in front of strangers. He said, 'I did *not* have the map upside down,' in a sort of quiet, strangled voice. I tried to be tactful. I said, 'We're all hopeless with maps. Once you get to know the moor you find your way by landmarks: St. Dinas's spire, the estuary, the plantations and the hills. The Jacksons are the best at it, they're brilliant even in fogs.'

'Why don't you come with us,' suggested Jane. The Hamiltons looked at each other doubtfully, then Felix said, 'No, we've *got* to learn to find our own way.' As we parted and rode on I heard Huw's voice saying sadly, 'I wish we'd stayed with them; I know we're going to end up in a bog with you two in charge.'

'Snooty weren't they?' said Jane. 'Not a bit friendly. I knew they'd be stuck up, but their ponies were nothing special, were they?'

'They all looked nice agreeable ponies,' I said, 'and the sort that'll settle down all right on the moor.'

Louisa said, 'I'm sorry for that poor little Huw lost with his two quarrelling brothers.'

I thought about the Hamiltons as we rode on towards the dark ruined tower. Tall, thin and dark, Felix had a proud but worried look; Toby was sturdier and broader with a smooth, round, more complacent face and Huw's though perky and cheeky was also rather sad, I guessed he would be easy to wound. I wondered how we'd all get on with them. It was difficult to judge since we'd met them in the middle of a quarrel and anyway it looked as though they might decide to 'keep themselves to themselves', as we say in St. Dinas.

Old Mrs. Hinds, wearing a dressing-gown and

wheezing loudly, came to the door of her lonely stone cottage. She thanked us for our trouble and we said we hoped she'd soon be better and could we do any shopping for her. Mummy is always telling us to offer to do sick people's shopping. But Mrs. Hinds said that her son was shopping for her in his lunch hour and dropping it in that evening.

Relieved of responsibility and breakable medicine bottles we could do as we pleased, Louisa suggested taking Jane to see Tolkenny Castle, but I was against it; Redwing really hates the place. I'm sure she sees ghosts, and the local legend says that a curse on the Kenny family meant every heir is sent to an early death by the appearance of a white hare which generally caused the young man's horse to shy. I suppose it could have been a cover-up for the fact that Kennys were all atrocious riders and fell off for nothing, but I could see Misty swerving at the sight of a ghostly hare and Jane falling down the ramparts to an untimely end. She sat nicely, but I didn't trust her to stay on if anything went wrong; she didn't have that 'glued on' look of people who've ridden for years and years.

Anyway, we then realised that the weather was changing, the clear spring day had clouded over and it was going to rain, in fact it was raining at the other end of the moor and the spire of St. Dinas had already vanished into a grey mist. Jane looked at the rugged, brown moor before us and the grey void beyond and said rather nervously, that she thought we ought to hurry home as fast we could.

We decided to have a gallop while the visibility was still good and so we both instructed Jane at once on the importance of leaving the choice of path entirely to Misty, and how two people can't steer and once you start interfering your pony doesn't know whether he's in charge or not. Then we set off at a fairly sedate gallop. I divided my time between looking back, to make sure that Jane was still with us, and forward at the ominous grey mist that was rolling to meet us. Suddenly all warmth and light departed and we were enclosed in cold, clammy drizzle, in a tiny, eerie world of ourselves and the few yards of heather and stones that we could see. I slowed to a walk and from behind Jane asked in a quavery voice if I knew where we were. 'Yes, near Black Tor,' I shouted back. 'We haven't had time to get lost yet.' I was relying on Redwing and the rising ground of the Tor to keep me going in the right direction and soon we should meet the well-trodden path that led to the Jacksons' farm. We rode on and on in our wet grey prison. I was beginning to think that I must have lost my sense of direction and taken a wrong turn when suddenly we heard disembodied voices floating through the mist. At first I thought it was the Jacksons, but as we drew nearer and the voices separated and became distinct there were two angry ones wrangling and one tearful one sobbing and we all realised that it was the Hamiltons again.

We all began to shout, 'Hullo!' 'Are you lost?' 'Coo-ee.'

'Oh, thank goodness, it's those girls,' said Huw's voice. We went on calling and presently a small dark shape came out of the mist and he and his little dun pony seemed equally determined to join us. 'Neither of my brothers are much good with that map,' he said, wiping his eyes on the cuff of his anorak. 'We've spent the whole day lost. I've definitely decided against being an explorer.' Then Felix and Toby joined us reluctantly.

'One *ought* to be able to find one's way home with a compass,' Felix said angrily, 'even in a fog. It's ridiculous ...'

'But none of the paths run straight in any direction for more than a few yards,' I pointed out. 'You can't just charge due east. Your pony trips over a boulder or falls in a bog. If we were on a smooth sandy desert or huge grass plain it would be much easier.' But Felix remained disgruntled. Toby asked, 'Are we heading towards Penhydrock?' When Louisa answered, 'No, for the Jacksons', Black Tor Farm, then it's easy — you just go along the road.' I knew that she had seen what I had seen, the nice wide, well hoof-marked path which led to the Jacksons' wall. I shouted back, 'Can Huw jump?' Felix said, 'Yes,' but Huw shouted, 'My highest's three-feet-one.' And Louisa added, 'We'll come last. I'll give him a lead.' I jumped the wall and stopped but Felix and Toby went past me like a cavalry charge and vanished into the suddenly thinning mist. Jane lurched over in slow-motion and then Spider, followed by the little dun, hopped over neatly and calmly. Felix and Toby came back looking rather shamefaced and they both jumped the second wall under control, which was just as well for Tracy came running to meet us at the yard gate, calling, 'Be careful, Heather's on Speedwell and he's never been ridden before.'

We dismounted and made our ponies creep into the yard to watch. Speedwell was a bright bay with white socks and a wide blaze and Mick held her carefully as he pursuaded her forward a few steps at a time. Heather sat very light and still in the saddle and Tracy stood ready to hand out rewards from a scoop of oats. As Speedwell tottered forward her eyes on the scoop, she staggered under the unaccustomed weight and looked quite incapable of bucking, rearing or putting up any sort of fight, but I'd watched the Jacksons back ponies before and had seen how sudden movements or un-expected noises could turn them into terrified wild animals determined to get rid of the monster on their backs, so I shushed everyone bossily and told them they *must* keep still.

When the tottering circuit of the yard was completed, Heather dismounted carefully, and then the Jacksons all made a tremendous fuss of Speedwell, who looked surprised but pleased. Then we introduced the Hamiltons and they and Jane all began to ask questions about breaking-in. Heather explained that she and Mick had four to break: Speedwell, Strongbow, Drummer and Dickon, and that Dad had expected them to be reliable enough to carry trekkers by June. They'd backed all three of the big ones, but little Dickon was still nervous of his saddle so they were lunging him in it.

I could see that the Hamiltons were impressed by Heather and that they liked the look of Mick, so when I asked if the Jacksons would be free to ride to Menacoell next day I also suggested to Felix that if they wanted to see North Moor they should come too.

Heather said, 'It's too far for any of the youngsters, but if we ride them first and tell Dad that the others need a long ride or two to get them really fit before the season starts, yes, we'll manage it.'

'Carolyn and William back?' asked Mick.

'Tonight,' I told him. 'They broke up two days ago but they were going to London to see the sights and plays and things.'

'And we'll all take food to cook?' asked Louisa.

'I'm boiling the eggs at home,' said Mick firmly, remembering a disaster from last summer.

We agreed to meet at the Jacksons' at ten and all ride over to the Mitchells'. Heather said that they would meet us at the bottom of the lane, ten sharp, but, knowing them, I rather doubted this. Then as the weather was getting steadily worse and a cold grey rain had begun to fall heavily, we all set off for home at a brisk trot. We dropped Jane and a very bedraggled Misty at Chapel Cottages, and said 'Goodbye' to the Hamiltons at our gate. As we hurried the ponies into the stable Louisa said, 'I hope those boys won't spoil tomorrow by arguing.'

THREE

My doubts proved right, there was no sign of the Jacksons at the end of the lane. It was an improving morning; one of those days that look rather dreary when you first get up and then the sky lightens and the sun makes longer and longer appearances and by lunchtime it's a marvellous day.

Jane had arrived at our house early, with Misty looking dazzlingly perfect again, and found Louisa and me still knocking the worst off our mud-encrusted ponies and arguing about what we were taking for lunch. But we were ready by the time the Hamilton hoofs were heard clattering up the road. Then we all met with disappointment − no Jacksons.

For a bit we waited, sitting in the pale sunlight and letting the ponies graze on the delicious spring grass they had found at the side of the road. Then we decided to go and see what was happening for, as Louisa said, the Jacksons are subject to last minute panics and sometimes extra people are a help.

There seemed to be a major panic in progress and everyone was screaming at everyone else, except for

Mick who was trying to bridle Silver Sand who hates having his ears touched and was upset by the general racket. We sent Felix in to help him because height is a great advantage when it comes to bridling. Louisa went to help Tracy who was screaming at Pirate and holding her side where he'd just bitten her, while tears ran down her face. Though Louisa is only about a year older than Tracy she's a much more determined character and Pirate recognised this at once and submitted to being groomed without further fuss.

I found Heather who was grooming Crackers and arguing with her father who had apparently taken Bell-boy's saddle, which she had cleaned specially, and given it to the trekker who was to ride Trudy. 'You *know* that great saddle of hers will be right down on Bellboy's withers,' complained Heather angrily.

'Be all right with a couple of foam bath mats underneath,' said Mr. Jackson unmoved. 'Better than sending a customer out with a dirty saddle.'

'She'll ruin it, stretch it out of shape, so that it's no good for the narrow ponies.'

'I'll clean the dirty one,' I suggested. 'Won't take more than five minutes. Where is it?'

'Tack room,' said Heather, 'You'll know it, some daft trekker dropped it in a puddle and it could only fit Trudy.'

It was a very wide old-fashioned sort of saddle, which looked as though it had been specially made for a cart-horse and an outsize rider, and it really was re-voltingly dirty. I could see why even Mr. Jackson, who sees nothing wrong with rusty bits and pink foam bath mats, had drawn the line at it. I cleaned away and

Jane appeared towing Redwing and Misty to see what I
was doing and promptly offered to take over. I refused. I
felt sure that her standards would be far too high and
we would all be held up for hours while she polished it
to perfection. I was just doing it well enough to pass
Mr. Jackson. As soon as it was done I rushed it across
to him and then went to take Redwing. The Jacksons
were putting on their crash caps — they never wore
them until Daddy gave Mrs. Jackson a lecture on the
horrors of brain damage. He's terribly bossy about
safety measures and will tell off complete strangers in
the most embarrassing way. At last we were ready and
we set off down the lane at a brisk trot for we were
going to be terribly late at the Mitchells'. To reach
Chilmarth by road you have to go along two sides of a
triangle. On ponies you simply cross the St. Dinas
road on to Middle Moor and then ride diagonally towards the Redbridge road.

The Mitchells' is rather a grand farm. It's on the
eastern edge of the moor where the land becomes flat
and fertile and borders the estuary. It's the sort of farm
that has a dairy herd and great dutch barns and silage
pits and corn driers, the sort of farm where the farmer
grows rich; entirely different from the hard-won fields
and the acres of heather and boulder that Mr. Jackson
struggles with at Black Tor.

We'd put Mick in the lead because Silver Sand is
young and wild and not always easy to control in
company. Then Felix on his dark brown Minstrel,
who has black points and no white markings, not even
a star. Then Heather on Bellboy, whom she has been
schooling for two years and is now really well-trained,

then Toby on his stout skewbald, Patchwork, then me and Jane and Louisa and Huw and finally Tracy on the villainous Pirate who was already out of control and making darting attacks on Huw's Biscuit in order to bite her rump.

It was rather difficult suddenly having so many new people and I couldn't help worrying how William, who's a critical character, would get on with the four newcomers; it might spoil everything if he took a violent dislike to one of them.

The nearer we came to Chilmarth the worse my worries grew until they entirely spoiled my pleasure in the fine morning, in the wet earthy smell of spring, in the moor and the fields spread before us, the sun glinting on the narrow channel of water in the estuary and in Redwing's long smooth stride as we cantered along the twisting, slightly downhill path. I began to feel certain that things would turn out badly. We came to the edge of the moor and turned left up a wide peaty track; young green fronds of bracken unfurled on either side of us, flocks of seagulls circled and cried above newly ploughed fields. We bunched together and began to talk. I told Felix and Toby that William had a new horse that none of us had seen, but Carolyn had written from school to tell me that he was a sensible bay called Brutus, up to weight, with a slightly Roman nose and hoofs like soup plates.

Chilmarth is long and low and built of stone. It's a larger and nicer house than either Rosebank or Black Tor Farm and it has roses and Wistaria and other creepers growing all over it and looks really great in summer. Inside it's rather too smart and highly polished except for the farmhouse kitchen which has a flagstone floor and is suitable for dogs and people in gumboots.

We didn't go in because William and Carolyn were waiting, ready, mounted and rather cross, in the farm-yard. I hastily pointed out Jane and the Hamiltons and they all looked at each other with apparent dislike. Then we rode out of the front gate, across the road and on to North Moor in a slightly disagreeable silence.

The worst of people going away to school is that you start every holiday as strangers and as we rode I looked critically at William and Carolyn. Except for having grown, they didn't seem to have changed much, but I was struck anew by their wide, soft, well-fed looking faces and their size. They and Jane Shaw are large for their ages, Louisa and I are small and the Jacksons about normal. I looked at the Hamiltons and decided that they were normal too.

The day was still improving, and as we rode up the lower slopes of Menacoell we started to cook in our anoraks. The St. Dinas ponies were beginning to tire, Pirate had stopped his attacks on Biscuit, Silver Sand and Minstrel no longer fought for their heads, but were content to amble along on loose reins. I inspected Brutus. He was large and plain and solid and his soup-plate hoofs were obviously tortured by stones. He looked like an elderly gentleman with corns whenever he crossed a really rough patch of ground. The Mitchells have never gone in for real moorland ponies, perhaps because they were always large for their ages or possibly because Mr. Mitchell likes them to look smart. As they have a farm horse-box they can go to more shows and rallies than the rest of us, who can't face hacking all

those miles and miles to civilisation very often. Carolyn's
Zephyr is a part-bred Arab with long white socks and
the sort of legs that chip easily, so in our wild country
the socks are always spoiled by trickles of blood and
pink scabs.

Half-way up Menacoell we stopped to give our ponies
a breather and to let the stragglers catch up. We turned
to look at the view; we could see the sea and the
estuary and Chilmarth's green fields, an oasis on the
edge of the brown, grey moor.

'What's this hill called?' Felix asked.

'Menacoell. The top is the highest point on the moor,'
William told him. And I added, 'It's supposed to mean
Stone of the Hawk.' Jane arrived leading Misty. 'She's
terribly tired,' she told us in a worried voice.

'Don't you believe it.' Heather sounded very certain.
'She's bone lazy, always has been. Look, all the others
have got here and she's one of the fittest, Dad's been
riding her all winter.'

'Perhaps I'm too heavy for her?'

Mick and Heather laughed. 'Of course you're not,
she's a real weight-carrier; look at her chest. No, she's
just a sleepy sort of pony that likes a quiet life and
plenty to eat. Left to herself she'd burst! Dad says she's
a real 'good doer'. He likes them like that; Mick and I
would rather have the goers.'

Everyone except Tracy agreed that they liked goers,
and then Heather made Jane remount and we climbed
on up the ever-steepening slope of Menacoell. I heard
Toby asking Mick if we were going to the very top
and Mick explaining that we couldn't, not on the ponies.

There were too many rocks and large boulders, they could break a leg. 'We're taking you to a place we know. It was the old shepherd's cottage. We camped there last summer.'

Suddenly I was seized with dread. Wasn't this a very stupid thing we were doing, revealing to these new-comers our own special place? Supposing we turned out to be incompatible and became enemies instead of friends? It was my fault, I'd suggested it, but now I realised that we ought to have shown them all the ordinary places first and made sure that we liked them, before revealing the secrets of Menacoell.

We'd reached the edge of the terrace where the little stream, flowing more slowly, had time to widen into a pool. Our ponies knew the place and hurried towards it, ears pricked, eager for their long, delicious drink. When they'd all finished we rode along the terrace, a small, flat shelf of land sticking out of the hillside, towards the stone-walled sheep pens and the one-storeyed cottage, which we considered our own. We had our family pens and the ponies knew where they belonged. Misty went in with the Jacksons'. As soon as our ponies were safely imprisoned and greedily grazing the short spring grass, we all went to see what could be fixed up for the Hamiltons. There was a nice large pen we'd all rejected as too much work the summer before, but now we were all larger and stronger, especially William and Mick, and with two good-sized Hamiltons to help it no longer looked such an impossible job to build up the broken-down wall. We all began heaving stones energetically and Jane and

Toby became terribly efficient at fitting them into the
wall. We heaved and heaved until finally even Felix
agreed that Minstrel would stay in.

By this time we were starving and our thoughts
were all of lunch. We decided that as it was a lovely
day we'd use our outside fireplace and Mick and I
rushed to get wood, while the others took the new-
comers to see the cottage and to find the frying pan
and other useful objects we keep hidden away there.
Moors are not usually very good places for finding
wood, but we had a stack of rotting sheep hurdles and
broken doors to keep us going and when that ran out
we'd decided we'd have to bring up spades and dig
peat. Mick had just got the fire alight (we'd built a
stone fireplace in a grassy hollow between three flat-
topped rocks which could be used as seats, but we keep
them as tables and backrests) when there was a lot of
indignant noise and everyone else came rushing out of
the cottage.

'People have been *living* there,' said Carolyn.

'Ugh, cigarette ends everywhere,' added Louisa.

'We'll soon put a stop to that,' William sounded
very firm. 'A good stout padlock.'

'Wouldn't stop them,' said Mick. 'They've only
got to break a pane of glass; now if there were
shutters ...'

It seemed best to eat and everyone began to produce
food. Louisa and I had brought apples and eleven rather
squashed sausages which Carolyn, who had taken over
the frying pan, began to cook. The Jacksons had
brought masses of hard-boiled eggs and bread and
butter, Jane sandwiches and a packet of biscuits, and

the Mitchells had raided the deep freeze for fishcakes and hamburgers which had arrived unsquashed in their proper saddle bags. Felix produced a magnificent pork pie from his knapsack and we decided to start on that and the eggs while everything else was cooking. Felix began to carve up the pie and Toby immediately started to interfere and tell him he was doing it all wrong. Felix said he wasn't, and so when it turned out that he *had* cut it into ten slices instead of eleven it was all rather awkward and he became cross and said he didn't want any, he was going to see if Minstrel was all right, and walked off.

'Sulking as usual,' said Toby complacently.

'Anyone would sulk who had you as a younger brother,' remarked William in his coldest and most squashing voice. Poor Huw, looking from Toby, red-faced and squashed, to Felix's lonely and retreating back, obviously didn't know which brother to support. The atmosphere was horrid. I said that I was going to inspect the cottage and wandered away taking alternate bites of egg and pie and wishing that we'd never set eyes on the Hamiltons.

We'd left the cottage tidy and carefully swept with our one balding broom, but now there was a cardboard box overflowing with bottles and coke cans and jagged lidded baked bean tins. A dirty sock lay abandoned in a corner, cigarette ends and spent matches scattered the floors. It was all very depressing and it seemed odd too because we don't usually get many campers early in the year, the moor's too bleak. And then people don't normally climb Menacoell from the south, for only the northern path is marked on the map, and so the cottage, grey stone, against grey stone, remains unnoticed on its terrace, known only to the locals.

From behind me Mick's voice said, 'May have been just a couple of walkers who got lost or found their tent too cold.'

'Let's hope the fire smoked and put them off ever coming back,' I said, looking at the half-burnt wood in the grate.

Mick looked up the chimney and then came out grinning. 'The starlings have been at it again. Oh well, they'll have hatched by the time *we* want a fire.'

'It doesn't seem worth clearing up if people can just walk in,' I said sadly. 'Don't you think William's padlock would do any good?'

'It would keep out the law-abiding, but they wouldn't use the cottage unless they needed shelter urgent-like. If this lot came back a padlock would just annoy them and we'd have a broken window as well as a mucky cottage.' Then we heard Heather's voice calling, 'Food!' Outside we saw Felix also making his way slowly towards the fire. We converged on him and asked if Minstrel had settled down, then we went back together.

Carolyn's cooking smelled and tasted delicious. We had taken the plates and knives and forks home at the end of the summer so we sandwiched the hamburgers and, waiting until the sausages and fishcakes had cooled a bit, we ate them in our fingers. When we'd eaten we all felt much more agreeable and we began to tell the Hamiltons and Jane about the funny and the awful things that had happened when we camped. Then Jane told us about riding near London and her friend who had two showjumpers and a gymkhana pony and how everyone wore black coats even at pony club rallies. The Hamiltons said it wasn't quite as bad where they had lived, but nearly everyone had trailers and you hardly ever hacked. 'I think we'll like it a lot better here,' Felix said, stretching out on the short turf. 'Well, once we've learned the way around.'

'Dad was furious that we kept getting lost yesterday,' Huw told us. 'He said we were incompetent halfwits. Of course he can find his way *anywhere*. He's explored miles and miles of unmapped territory.'

'And it wasn't fair,' said Toby angrily. 'Felix wouldn't let me have the map until we were hopelessly lost and the fog had come down, so I didn't have a chance to be competent. Next time *I'm* going to start with the map and I bet I don't make half the mess Felix did.'

'No, of course not, we all know you're the brilliant little explorer,' said Felix in a sarcastic and muffled voice – his face was hidden in his arms.

'Of course unmapped territory would make it a lot easier.' Heather ignored the Hamilton bickering. 'I mean wherever you turned up you'd discover somewhere, and if there's no map no one can tell you you didn't go the best way.'

'And maps don't always work on the moor,' I added. 'It's an eerie place. The old people tell stories of piskies stealing a traveller's sense of direction and letting him go round and round till he drops.' Then, seeing that Toby was about to be sarcastic over Felix and the piskies, I hastily embarked on the story of the pedlar who, years and years ago, tried to cross West Moor in

a blizzard. He was never seen again and was thought to
have been sucked down into the depths of Barley Bog,
as were many a careless sheep and cow and pony
before the plantation dried it out. And now the old
man's ghost is said to haunt the firs and on wild nights
a grey, glimmering figure, carrying a pedlar's tray
wanders moaning among the straight, tall trees.

When I had finished Carolyn said, 'Oh shut up,
Frances, you know I hate creepy stories.'

'So do I,' agreed Huw. 'I would have blocked my
ears if she'd gone on much longer.'

'My sister! said William contemptuously. 'She
screams at spiders too; if there's one in the bath *I* have
to go in and get it out.'

'Lots of people have phobias, it's quite normal,'
remarked Felix. 'Only girls are allowed to shriek and
make a fuss while boys are expected to hide theirs; it's
all a bit mad.'

'You can be cured of silly ones quite easily,' Louisa
spoke with authority because she is always discussing
medical matters with Daddy, 'but agoraphobia, when
you're afraid to go out of your house, it sounds
awful.'

Heather and Jane were discussing Misty. 'I don't
think she's the right pony for you,' Heather was
saying. 'Now you're going to ride every day you'll
improve a lot and you could do with something livelier
already.'

'But she's so sweet. She's got such a lovely, gentle
nature. I'm terribly fond of her already.'

'Yes, but you don't want to land yourself with a
pony that's a bit slow and not much of a jumper.'

'I do wish someone would buy Pirate,' wailed Tracy. 'Dad keeps saying I've got to persevere with him, but I know he's never going to get any better, not with me.'

'All he needs is a good wallop,' announced Mick sitting up and looking hopefully round the debris of plastic bags and boxes. 'Anything left to eat?'

FOUR

Jane arrived earlier than ever next morning, and when Louisa and I, still eating breakfast, groaned loudly at this excess of energy Mummy went out and we could hear her asking if Mrs. Shaw liked working in Baybourne and whether the buses ran at convenient times and how the decorating was going? It's extraordinary how grown-ups can spin out that sort of conversation. It was a lovely spring morning with warm and balmy air smelling of gorse and primroses, and when we'd said hullo to Jane we went down the field to catch our ponies. They'd finished their breakfasts and were reclining in the sun. They'd looked so comfortable lying side by side that we decided to let them have a rest and walk to Black Tor. So we loved them for a bit and then we set off walking beside Jane. She was in a very chatty mood and went on and on about her friends at the riding school near London. She told us all about the ponies they rode and the prizes they won, but it wasn't very interesting to us as we'd never set eyes on any of them.

Peace seemed to reign at the Jacksons'. The dogs,

collies and terriers, who swept round us in a sort of
tidal wave, all had smiling faces and wagging tails so
we knew that for once there was no row or panic in
progress.

We found Heather and Mick out on the moor. They
were already at work in the 'school', a flat space they
had cleared for themselves, piling the stones into a low
wall in the traditional manner, because every one of
their fields was needed for grazing or hay until July and
by that time the trekkers had taken over the ponies and
there was no chance to school them.

Mick was lunging Heather on Strongbow, he was
dun, a larger version of Biscuit, so we approached
cautiously. Seeing us, they stopped lunging and Heather
dismounted carefully.

'Dad's gone to Baybourne to pick up a spare part
for the milking machine, but he says you can try any
pony you fancy,' she told Jane. Jane said she'd like to
have another go on Crackers and as he, by some mir-
acle, was in the stable we all went back to the farm
buildings to collect our mounts. I was given Drummer, a
solid, sleepy piebald with masses of whiskers, to
school and Louisa was to be lunged on the tiny grey,
Dickon.

'Tracy's supposed to be riding him,' Heather explained, 'but she'd rather help Mum indoors and then
Dad gets furious because he wants the pony quiet by
the summer.'

As I sat on the sleeping Drummer and watched Jane
hopping round and round Crackers who wouldn't stand
to be mounted, I thought how awful it must be to be
born into a really horsey family if you weren't horsey

by nature. It seemed bad luck that Jane hadn't a farming father when she was horsemad and all the Jackson ponies were wasted on Tracy. Then as Jane was still hopping and Crackers still twirling, I offered to hold him, but Jane gritted her teeth and said, 'No. I'm *going* to do it by myself.' The hopping went on and on and at last, when we were all ready, Mick rescued her. Mick was back on Strongbow, and as we rode soberly to the school I asked him what I was supposed to be teaching Drummer.

'The aids,' he said, 'for walking, trotting, stopping and turning. That's all. He's not ready to canter yet and anyway he doesn't need to, not for trekkers.'

Some people find schooling boring, but I've always enjoyed teaching ponies new things, the feeling of triumph when you get something into their heads and the slow steady improvement which comes as they grow stronger and their muscles develop. Drummer had rather a thick head but by using plenty of voice as well as legs and hands I got him to understand what I meant about going faster and slower. Turning was more difficult. It was rather like manoeuvring a huge ship. Mostly his neck turned but not the rest of him. Mick was practising the same sort of things on Strongbow, and in the centre of the school Heather was lunging Louisa round and round on Dickon. Jane had agreed to take Crackers for a little hack.

Time passed and all was going well when we heard the rapid drumming of flat-out galloping hoofs. We all dismounted hastily. It wasn't cowardice, just that experienced horsebreakers like the Jacksons are very careful not to turn ponies into bucking broncos or mad bolters by letting them get over excited or out of control before they've learned the aids. Then Jane and Crackers came in view, hurtling along the twisting path. Jane's crash cap had gone, her dark hair stood out round her head, and she shouted, 'Whoa, whoa! Crackers, will you whoa!' as she tugged on the reins. She whirled past us and vanished through the open gate into the farmyard. We listened and presently we heard scolding noises and then she came riding back.

'He behaved beautifully until I turned for home, then he simply *wouldn't* stop. I tugged for all I was worth. I'll take him straight back and *make* him behave.'

'Don't let him out of a collected canter,' advised Heather.

'You've lost your crash cap,' Louisa pointed out accusingly.

'Yes, I'll go and get it.' Jane cantered away and we began to school again. Soon we heard angry scoldings and cries of 'Crackers, *will* you stand!' and we were just debating which of us should go to the rescue when the hoofs began to drum again and Crackers came up the path this time with Jane half on. I hate seeing people half on because when they do let go they have a horrid habit of falling all among their ponies' galloping hoofs. I tried to go in pursuit, but in the excitement Drummer had forgotten what aids meant and just stood gazing after Crackers. I'm sure his mouth would have been open if horses opened their mouths in amazement, but of course they don't. Meanwhile Strongbow had started bucking and, not being used to the weight of a rider, he'd overbalanced and he and Mick were rolling

about on the ground. We all forgot Jane and rushed to
the assistance of Mick. He was all right. He said that
with luck Strongbow had given himself such a fright
he'd never dare buck again. I looked round for Jane.
She came riding out of the farmyard, muddy but firmly
in the saddle.

Heather shouted, 'Not again. You're upsetting the
youngsters.'

'I can't help it, I'm *not* giving in,' Jane shouted
back.

'She's a menace,' complained Heather. 'Look, let's
take them all into the yard and then we'll get her back
on Misty and go for a little hack.'

'We'd just reached the yard gate when we heard the
familiar sounds. Strongbow was trembling wild-eyed
and upset. Dickon twirled round entangling himself in
the lunge. Drummer only raised his heavy head and
pricked his ears as Crackers swerved round the stone
gatepost, skidded across a strip of concrete and stopped
dead at the stable door. Jane, half-way up his neck, slid
slowly to the ground.

Heather grabbed Crackers's reins. 'We're going to
take the youngsters for a very quiet ride,' she said.
'You can come if you like — on Misty.'

With Heather on Crackers the ride was a very sedate
one, mostly walking with an occasional trot, but quite
fun because the sun was shining and we went round
the bottom of Black Tor. As we came back to the farm
we could see three figures leaning against the gate and
as we drew nearer we identified them as Mrs. Jackson,
Tracy and our local policeman, Mr. Weston. Tracy
began to wave and shout so we stirred the weary four-

year-olds into a trot. 'There's someone lost!' she was calling. 'Come on, searchers needed.'

Mick groaned. 'They haven't started already?'

All through the summer the people who live on the moor are expected to turn out and search for lost visitors. No one minds when it's a real accident or mishap, but so often they've just been silly and wandered off in the wrong shoes and clothes, without a map and worst of all without a companion, and sometimes without telling a soul where they were going. I suppose they're so used to flat green parks that they don't realise that the moor is a wild place: a place where no one hears your cries and runs to pick you up. People see it in fine weather and become very enthusiastic about the beauties of nature and all that, but, as anyone who has lived in the *real* country knows, nature is moody and cruel and often dangerous, 'red in tooth and claw', as the saying goes.

Mr. Weston was saying, 'A man called Carter. In his forties, five-foot-ten, medium build. His wife rang us late last night to say he hadn't returned, but she'd no idea where he'd gone. We found his car this morning, parked at the top of the surgery lane, so it looks as though he's been out all night.'

'You reckon he's injured?' asked Mick.

'Must be,' said Heather. 'It's easy to wander round in circles in the dark, but if he started walking when it got light he'd have reached a telephone by now, surely?'

I looked at Louisa. 'We'll get our ponies and ride over to St. Crissy and back,' I offered.

'If you would, we're stretched, but they are sending a search party up from Baybourne this afternoon.

Trouble is that it's a busy time of year for the farmers and people won't turn out to look for a grown man like they will for a lost child.'

'We'll go over the top of Black Tor and back up the Baybourne side,' said Mick. 'The Mitchells are off somewhere, aren't they, Frances?'

'Yes, but the Hamiltons might help.'

'Old Dog?' asked Mick.

'I'd let the police party do that,' said Mrs. Jackson. 'It's too rough up the top there for ponies.'

'If Louisa and I ride down the middle track, Felix and Toby could do the lane and the southern edge. They know that bit.'

'They'll get lost.' Louisa sounded resigned.

Jane asked, 'Can I come with you Burnetts?'

'Yes, if you're riding Misty.'

Mr. Weston gave us a lift home in his police car and we rushed in to tell Mummy and grab some lunch. There was a note for us. *Miss Gurney taken ill so I'm standing in for her. Beef steak pie and veg in oven. Ice cream in fridge. Leave some for Daddy. Back about six.* 'Poor Mummy,' I said, 'she's always standing in for someone. I wonder what's wrong with Gurney?'

'Measles, I expect.'

'She's about forty-five, she must have had them.' Miss Gurney is the receptionist and secretary at the health centre and works for all the doctors, so it's always a major catastrophe if anything happens to her. Mrs. Cole, the dispenser, is married with small children and only works part-time, which means that one of the doctors' wives has to rush in and man the telephone, and somehow it usually seems to be Mummy.

We ate quickly, put our plates in the dishwasher, and wrote a note about the vanished Mr. Carter. Then we got out the small first-aid rucksack. Daddy always keeps two ready stocked for emergencies. They're full of useful things: a flashing torch, a plastic sheet and a light-weight blanket as well as brandy and all the usual first aid stuff. We put provisions in our pockets and then Louisa said she would make a thermos of tea while I rang the Hamiltons. I said we didn't need tea and she said Mr. Carter might, but I think really it was just an excuse to get out of the telephoning.

I got Mrs. Hamilton who sounded nice and was very concerned about Mr. Carter being out all night. She said that Huw could hardly move after the marvellous trek we'd taken him yesterday but that she was sure Felix and Toby would want to help. She fetched a pen and wrote down exactly where they were to search and where the nearest telephones would be if they found him. That reminded me to collect some more telephone money for us. We might need to ring our parents and not just 999.

Of course Jane arrived before we were ready. She helped us groom, but I think she was rather shocked by our sketchy ways. We only bother with the saddle mark in emergencies.

As we hurried up the road she would go on and on about 'her dreadful exhibition on Crackers' and what a bad rider she was. We'd already forgotten the morning's incidents and our minds were on looking for Mr. Carter, so, though we did our best to console her, it was a relief to turn on to the moor and start the search. We explained that we had to spread out and ride in line towards the hump and tower of Tolkenny Castle, and that if Mr. Carter wasn't wearing a bright anorak, he would be very difficult to see lying among the heather, so we would have to look very hard and shout his name at intervals, in case he wasn't unconscious, but just lying there with a broken leg. We would also have to keep quiet in between shouts and listen in case he was calling for help.

We separated — Louisa nearest to Black Tor, me to Old Dog and Jane in the centre. We rode slowly. We called, we listened, we looked for a prostrate form among the grass and the heather and the outcrops of rock. I tried to work out what Mr. Carter meant to do. The best reason for parking in the surgery lane was that you intended to climb Old Dog. It's not really a climb, but the last bit is quite a rocky scramble, and a lot of visitors go up him and Menacoell.

Well, if he was still on Old Dog the police would find him, but supposing he'd been tempted by the sight of Black Tor or the distant view of Tolkenny? Then we might find him collapsed somewhere along our route; from the Barley Bog plantation onwards the likelihood of our finding him would grow greater.

We didn't actually go in the plantation, because there's no reason to trip or fall in there, just a very wet centre ride, and I didn't think anyone would leave the moor on a fine, sunny day to walk through a dark, dank wood. We shouted and listened and then rode on. It was becoming more and more difficult to make one's eyes search efficiently. Mine were refusing to concentrate. I tried shaking my head and then making them focus on special objects: a bird that looked like a cuckoo, a patch of the parasitic plant, pink and pretty, but rightly named Lousewort, fresh green grass forcing its way through the old yellow and brown tussocks. I began to call 'Mr. Carter' more often to make up for my eyes. We met no one, no farmers looking at their livestock, no walkers, no riders and we saw no sign of other searchers. We saw plenty of birds and rabbits, cattle, sheep and ponies and as we came up towards St. Crissy we met a little herd of ponies with three brand new foals.

Eventually we came to where the moor narrows and ends in the stone-walled farms of St. Crissy. We met on the lane that leads up to the village.

'Now what?' asked Jane, looking at me.

I pointed at the towering castle ruins. 'We'd better brave the ghosts and make sure he's not up there.'

'Oh yes, let's; I don't mind ghosts at all.'

'Redwing does.'

'I don't think Spider believes in them,' said Louisa. 'I'm sure he won't mind going first.'

We went through the gate beside the cattle grid and then we left the lane and took the steep track to the castle. Sheep grazed the green hill and the old fortifications of inner and outer ditches. On top the wind blew strong and cold, but you could see for miles: the sea, the moor, the estuary, the more wooded country to the west. Jane gazed in admiration. Louisa and I shouted, 'Mr. Carter'.

As we crossed the filled portion of the inner ditch into the ruins, Redwing began to snort and look about nervously with large eyes. I kept a sharp watch for white hares as well as for Mr. Carter.

From a distance the castle looks very real but close at hand it's a bit disappointing. So many of the walls have fallen it's difficult to picture it as it was in the old days. The dungeons have been carefully fenced off, and there are a host of green litter bins and notices forbidding you to climb on the walls. We shouted 'Mr. Carter', but the wind snatched the words and whisked them away. Louisa dismounted and peered through the mesh grilles into the dungeons. I looked into the ruined tower and persuaded Redwing through the labyrinth of broken walls. When we'd all convinced ourselves there was no one there we decided to search the ditches. Redwing, delighted to be out of the actual castle, plunged down into the ditch with no fuss at all. Spider followed, and then we realised that Jane, unused to precipitous slopes, was dithering on the top. 'Come on,' I called, 'just give Misty her head.' Then we both shrieked, 'Lean forward', as Jane came down with the backward seat.

The ditch was warm and grassy with primroses and thorn bushes, very peaceful compared with all the bloody fighting that must have gone on in it years ago. I'd begun to trot along it when, suddenly, Redwing shied, one of those real spin round on the hocks shies, and, with me half off, crashed into Spider. Louisa and I cracked our legs together. I spent some time rubbing my leg and apologising before I picked up the reins and turned Redwing back. She was still reluctant and snorting at something under a thorn bush — a bundle of clothes, or was it? 'Mr. Carter?' I called, and the bundle moved reluctantly. Redwing prepared for flight. 'Mr. Carter?' The bundle moved again. Slowly and painfully it sat up. A bruised and battered face streaked with dried blood peered at me, trying to see out of tiny eyes. 'Who are you?' he asked through swollen lips.

'Part of a search party looking for you,' I said, dismounting and taking off the first-aid rucksack, for, even if it wasn't Mr. Carter, he looked badly in need of first aid. Redwing had calmed down now that she recognised him as a real if battered man. I left her to graze.

Louisa, who had abandoned Spider, joined me. 'No brandy,' she said. 'He looks as though he may have hit his head.' I got out the thermos. He wasn't actually bleeding any more so there was no rush to do anything about his wounds. 'Have you been here all night?' I asked.

'Yes.' The sight of the thermos was having a reviving effect on him. He sat up a bit more and put out a hand to take the tea. He drank slowly; obviously his lips hurt.

'Are you Mr. Carter?' Louisa asked.

'Yes, Mr. damfool Carter,' he said bitterly. 'Who sent you to look for me?'

'The police,' I answered, offering biscuits and chocolate. Louisa was looking up at the castle wall. 'Did you fall from there?' she asked.

He looked up too. 'Yes, must have done, mustn't I?'

'You don't really remember?'

'No, I expect I hit my head.' He put up a hand to feel his head and I saw that the hand was swollen and bruised and bloodstained. We gave him more tea and he began to eat the biscuits hungrily. I got out the blanket. 'We'll just cover you with this,' I said, 'and then one of us will go and telephone for an ambulance.'

'No, don't do that. I don't think I've done anything really serious.' He began to move his arms and legs cautiously, but when he tried to get up, he turned green and sank back quickly. 'It's my head,' he said in a faint voice, 'just my head.'

Louisa and I looked at each other. 'You go,' she said, 'you're better at explaining than I am. Jane and I will look after him.'

Mr. Carter peered up at me out of his battered face. 'Ring the police first, will you?' he asked. 'It's important that they should know I've been found.'

'Right, I'll do that.' I spread the blanket over him and offered the rucksack as a pillow. He seemed quite worn out with all the talking he'd done.

Jane had retired down the ditch and was grazing the three ponies. 'I thought I'd better get them out of the way,' she said, as I took Redwing. 'Is he all right?'

'He's not dying,' I said as I mounted, 'but he's very battered. I'm going to telephone for an ambulance. Help Louisa look after him.'

'I don't like accidents.'

'There's nothing to do, just go and keep her company.' I whizzed along the ditch, came out by the keep and went down the castle mound at a collected canter. I knew the telephone box was at the cross roads quite near Mrs. Hinds's cottage and it only took me a few minutes to reach it. It's always difficult to telephone and hold a pony − I think there ought to be rings to tie them to on country boxes − but Redwing seemed to sense an emergency, and when I shut the buckle of her reins in the telephone box door, she stood obligingly. I dialled nine, nine, nine and went through the tiresome business of saying where I was, then I got the police. I explained I was part of the search party and had found Mr. Carter and I thought he needed an ambulance. They said hang on and then they came back and said the radio cars in the vicinity were on their way and would I meet them at the ruins? Then they began to ask questions about how badly Mr. Carter was injured. I explained as best I could, but I could see Redwing was getting restless so I ended the conversation quickly.

I rode sedately back to the castle, shouted to Louisa from the edge of the inner ditch that they were on their way, and stationed myself on a nice patch of grass in front of the keep, and let Redwing graze. In a very short time I heard cars coming down the lane and saw blue lights flashing through the hedge. There seemed to be three police cars and soon a party of police came puffing up the steep track led by our own P.C. Weston.

'Hullo there,' he called. 'So you and your sister found him?'

'Yes, and Jane Shaw.'

'Frances Burnett,' he introduced me to the other policeman, 'our local Doctor's daughter.' Too out of breath from the hill to say much, they all nodded politely.

'He's down here,' I told them and led the way along the ditch.

'He hasn't moved or said anything since you went,' Louisa reported, 'but I think he's just resting.'

Two of the police knelt down beside him. The others

looked around. 'He seemed to think he might have
fallen from the wall,' I pointed. 'It doesn't seem very
likely. He's got such an awful face and hands, as though
he had been in a fight, I don't believe he'd have done it
falling on grass.'

The policemen looked at each other. 'Might have
scraped it on the wall,' one said.

'And crawled here to get out of the wind,' another
suggested.

'He'll remember what happened in a day or two, I
daresay,' said Mr. Weston comfortably. 'And now I
think we'd better get you girls on your way. It's getting
late, you've got a longish ride, and we don't want you
out on the moor in the dark.'

I asked about the blanket and the rucksack, knowing
that Daddy would hate to lose his first-aid arrange-
ments, and Mr. Weston said that he'd drop everything
in at Rosebank that evening. So we mounted and rode
for home. I was relieved that Mr. Carter was in more
responsible hands than mine, but Louisa was worried
lest the police should forget he had hit his head and
gave him brandy.

FIVE

The ponies were delighted to leave the problems and creepy atmosphere of Tolkenny ruins and when we reached the moor they set off for home at a brisk canter. We felt like tea too, so we let them speed along. Spider seemed to have much more breath than usual and even Misty felt quite lively in the cool evening air. We had decided to go home between the southern boundary and Old Dog in the hope of picking up the Hamiltons if they were still searching. We knew that the Jacksons, being experienced, would go straight home when they had searched their area and wait for news and instructions, but the Hamiltons, being new to it, might go on searching for hours.

We were past Old Dog and almost to the Ruveland lane when we heard a shout and saw a lone figure waving to us. It was Felix. 'We found him,' we called triumphantly. 'We've found him.' When we caught up with him we all explained at once about the inner ditch at Tolkenny and Mr. Carter's battered state and the police taking over, and when we'd finished Felix said, 'Well, that's great. I think I'll go home down the lane. It's a bit shorter and Minstrel seems tired after yesterday.'

'But where's Toby?' I asked. 'You weren't supposed to search alone.'

Felix's face turned slowly red. 'Oh, we had a row.' He tried to sound casual. 'He went off in a temper.'

'You're not very reliable searchers then,' I said in a cross voice, the irritation I'd been feeling over their constant quarrels suddenly bursting forth. 'The whole point is to go in twos at least, so that one can stay with the injured person and the other fetch help. It doesn't look as though Toby's even searching his area; didn't he realise that it was serious, that someone had been out all night?' Felix didn't answer but Louisa said, 'Oh, I do hope Toby isn't going to be lost now.'

'I expect he's home; he should be. He went off quite a long time ago,' Felix told her and then he rode in the direction of the lane without another word.

We rode on towards St. Dinas in an exhausted silence. I wondered if I had been too rude, whether the Burnetts and the Hamiltons would now be enemies for life instead of friends as I had hoped. But still, I comforted myself, we were better without them if they were going to spoil every expedition with their quarrels.

We parted from Jane on the road, and as we rode down the drive Mummy came rushing to meet us.

'Any luck?' she asked. As we unsaddled the ponies we told her how we'd found Mr. Carter.

'Oh, well *done*,' she said, 'but the poor man, out all night in that state. Are you starving? Would you like eggs for tea?' We said we would. We turned the ponies out and when they had drunk their fill we gave them each a huge and delicious feed as a reward for their part in the adventure.

We'd just sat down to our eggs and a great feast of cake and biscuits Mummy had produced from her store cupboard, when there was a knock at the back door. Louisa opened it revealing Felix and Minstrel. Felix looked very worried. 'Toby's not back,' he said, 'and there's no one at home. My father's in London and my mother and Huw seem to have gone off somewhere. I thought I'd better tell you that I was going to look for him.'

Mummy said, 'You can't go by yourself. We were just going to have tea. Look, put the pony in the stable and come and have tea, then if Toby's still not back we'll all search.'

Felix seemed quite relieved at being told what to do. I went out to the stable with him and we put Minstrel in Redwing's box and gave him water and a small feed — I was already wishing that I had not been quite so lavish to Redwing.

Mummy had boiled another egg but it wasn't a very chatty tea. I suppose Felix was worrying over Toby and I was regretting my plain speaking. Mummy kept the conversation going and Louisa told the story of how we'd found Mr. Carter all over again.

Afterwards we rang Penhydrock, but there was no reply, and then the Jacksons to tell them we'd found Mr. Carter but lost Toby and to ask if he had turned up there. They hadn't seen a sign of him.

We worked out a programme: Mummy and Louisa were to go to Penhydrock in the car and make sure that Toby wasn't there, then they would go up the lane to Black Dog and look there. I was to catch up Redwing and, if they weren't back in ten minutes, Felix and I were to search the moor towards St. Crissy.

'And don't be too tenacious,' Mummy said. 'We don't want to send out another party to look for you.'

As Mr. Weston hadn't appeared with the first-aid rucksack I got out the other one and as it's enormous, being Daddy's, Felix said he would take it. I felt very mean catching Redwing and told Felix that if anyone had to gallop for help it would be him, because she couldn't possibly do fast work after her enormous feed. I kept hoping that Mummy and Louisa would come racing up in the car to tell us Toby was home, but when the ten minutes were up, we knew he wasn't and that there was nothing for it but to go out in the cold evening air and search the moor *again*.

I felt really angry with Toby for causing all this trouble and I think it would have been fury, only it was tempered by fear that he had had an accident. I kept seeing him lying unconscious. Perhaps he'd fallen and hit his head on a rock. And would Patchy be standing over him like faithful horses in books, or would he have wandered off with a passing herd of ponies? I asked Felix what colour anorak his brother was wearing and it was a tiresome khaki parka, which we wouldn't have a hope of seeing among the heather at dusk.

The sun was setting, sinking lower and lower behind Tolkenny, silhouetting the ruins which rose grim and dark against the red and yellow sky. The moor stretched empty and gloomy; there was no sign of skewbald Patchy. We rode on into the dusk, calling, looking, listening. Gradually my eyes stopped focusing and my throat went dry in protest at all the calling it had done that day. I felt really fed up and I'm sure Redwing did too. Then the sun vanished below the horizon, the eastern sky gradually darkened, Tolkenny's tower faded from our view and the moor became wild and threatening.

Ahead great flocks of rooks were flying in to roost in the fir trees on Barley Bog, and their noisy cawing was a sort of comfort, drowning the small unidentifiable sounds of night. I shivered — it was really cold now that the sun had gone — and edged towards Felix. He had the torch. We converged as we came up to the plantation fence.

'Where can he have got to?' said Felix.

'He didn't suggest going up Old Dog?'

'No, Mum said the police were searching there.'

We rode round the corner of the plantation and came to the gate that opens on the centre ride. We stopped and looked in. It was pitch black inside, the firs sighed ominously in the breeze, and the settling rooks cawed sleepily. 'We'd better shout,' I said. 'Toby,' we yelled, 'Toby!' and the startled birds cawed and flapped above us. We waited and then we heard an answering shout. Felix yelled again and this time the answer came plainly, 'I'm here, in the wood.'

We looked down at the padlocked gate. 'He must have jumped.'

'All right in daylight, but a bit high and solid to jump in the dark.'

'Will it come off its hinges?' That was something I'd learned from the Jacksons.

'Brilliant!' said Felix dismounting. 'If you can hold the ponies I'll climb over and heave from the other side.'

It was a heavy gate and the hinges were welded with rust. We heaved and heaved, spurred on by Toby's plaintive shouts. He obviously thought we'd gone on without hearing him, and while we were heaving we had no spare breath with which to shout back. We heaved and rested and heaved again. Then at last we felt the hinges part. We lifted with all our strength and got the ringed parts high enough to free them from the hooks, lurching and staggering under the sudden extra weight. Then Felix came through to my side and we dragged it open. As we mounted we shouted, 'Coming', to comfort Toby.

'Something must be wrong,' said Felix in a worried voice. 'If he was just lost he'd have come to meet us by now.'

It was terribly dark in the wood so I reminded Felix about the torch and Redwing, who is very obliging about such things, stood absolutely still and let me have both hands to undo the rucksack straps and get it out.

With the torch's long beam ahead of us the plantation seemed less perilous though the going on the green grassy track was horribly deep, almost a bog in places. Felix shouted and Toby answered. He sounded near and straight ahead. I began to think of broken legs. I hoped it was a human leg as they are easier mended than ponies'. Suddenly the tip of the torch's beam picked out Patchy's stout skewbald frame. Minstrel neighed causing cawing and flapping above.

'Take care,' Toby called urgently, 'there's a terrible great bog somewhere there; I rode right into it. That's what did in his shoe.'

We could see the deep black holes where he had floundered through so we left the path and crept through the close-planted trees and came to Toby. 'What's up?' asked Felix.

'Look.' He picked up Patchy's near fore and showed us the grotesquely twisted shoe. 'He can't walk on it and I can't untwist it and it won't come off.' Toby sounded almost tearful and not at all his usual complacent self, but I suppose being alone in the Barley Bog Plantation at night was enough to unnerve anyone. He was also covered in mud.

'Did you fall off?' I asked, as I fumbled in the rucksack for cheering iron rations. Felix was using the torch to inspect the twisted shoe.

'Yes, I thought it was a lovely green ride and I came belting along at a gallop and went smack into that awful bog. Patchy fell on his head and I shot off into it. I suppose he trod on the shoe with his hind hoof when he tried to get out. He had an awful job.' Toby's spirits rose at the sight of the chocolate and he devoured it in a flash, except for two small bits I grabbed for Felix and myself. I felt we deserved something for coming to join him in his horrid predicament. Felix was tugging at the shoe without the least effect and Patchy stood, blowing down his neck and obviously grateful for all attempts at rescue.

Toby said, '*I* tried hammering it with a stone and pulling, but it wouldn't budge. Then I tried prising with a stick and the stick broke.'

I looked down into the torch's circle of light. 'We'll have to get those clenches up somehow; I've got a knife.' Felix had a better knife, one with a short screw driver, and we took it in turn to try to lever the clenches up. The worst of it was that it was quite a new shoe and the clenches were really tight. They hadn't even given on the twisted side and so a great piece of hoof had broken away with the shoe. I began to hate clenches after a bit — I mean they're always coming loose when you don't want them to; you've only got to plan a really long ride and you find your pony's a mass of risen clenches — yet those three beasts wouldn't rise whatever we did to them. It was so frustrating. We all knew enough about shoeing to realise that we had only to prise them up straight and the shoe would pull off as easy as anything, but could we get them up?

I said if we could get him to the Jacksons', they had a set of blacksmith's tools and Mick would have it off in a flash. But when we tried leading Patchy he obviously thought it quite impossible to put any weight on that foot and tried to hop along on three legs and he couldn't do that all the way to Black Tor Farm. Then I suggested that I rode to the farm and fetched the tools, but Toby pointed out that there was only one torch and Felix said it was ridiculous, 'We *must* be able to get the wretched thing off; we're not that feeble,' and he redoubled his prising efforts.

I visualised Charlie Cort, our blacksmith, taking off shoes. He puts the chisel-like end of the buffer against the clench and hits the buffer with his hammer until it cuts through the clench and when they're all cut through he levers the shoe off with the pincers. It's no trouble at all.

'We need a hammer,' I told Felix, 'then we could tap the knife as though it were a buffer.'

'Well we haven't got a hammer!' he shouted at me in irritation.

'I had a jolly good stone,' said Toby, feeling round in the dark. It was a good stone and I persuaded Felix to use it as a hammer. Toby held the hoof, I shone the torch and Felix hammered away, swearing when he missed. Patchy stood patiently and Redwing and Minstrel, who seemed to be getting rather friendly, stood close together, their heads towards the circle of light. After a lot of hammering and swearing Felix announced, 'This one's moving.' But it didn't seem to move much and the hammering went on and on and on. Felix wouldn't let anyone else take over. He kept saying, 'No, I've got the hang of it now,' and, 'It *is* my knife.' I controlled myself and didn't point out that the pony was Toby's and the torch a Burnett one. Eventually all three clenches were battered loose, if not actually up, and Felix began to tug at the shoe. Patchy didn't like this much, and without pincers of any sort it was difficult to get a grip, much less lever. Felix tugged and swore. Toby hung on to Patchy who pulled back and then gave a small indignant rear and suddenly the shoe came free. We all cheered. Patchy's hoof looked a bit of a mess but at least he could put it to the ground. 'I hope he's not lame,' said Toby anxiously.

'He could have sprained anything, galloping full tilt into a bog,' I pointed out. Felix put on the rucksack and I shone the torch as we led our ponies through the trees. Back on the track we mounted and Toby said Patchy *seemed* to be all right, so we tried a gentle trot down the ride. We squeezed out through the hinged end of the gate and then I held the ponies while the Hamiltons heaved it back. I switched on the red flashing part of the torch as they mounted in case anyone was out looking for *us*. It was lovely to set off for home. It seemed quite light now we were out of the wood. There were stars and a hazy moon and Old Dog looking friendly and familiar in the thin, pale light. We couldn't hurry over the stony ground because of Patchy's broken hoof, but Redwing put on her fastest walk and, at intervals, I flashed the torch to tell everyone that we were coming.

Relieved of their anxieties the Hamiltons began to bicker. The star that Felix said was Orion and his dagger, Toby said was the plough. They found rival Pole stars and called each other fools for not knowing the North from the South. In the end I got so fed up. I shrieked at them to stop it and said they ruined every ride we went on with their silly arguments. They shut up and we rode on in an uncomfortable silence. But I heard a fox bark and the long, weird calls of the hunting owls and, though the moor looked wild and strange, its mood had changed since dusk and it no longer threatened.

Presently a light came bobbing towards us and then there were cries of 'Have you got Toby?' Which we answered with cheerful shouts of 'Yes' and 'He's O.K.' It was Daddy and Mrs. Hamilton who had come to meet us. They seemed quite calm and said that they had decided to give us until ten before they mounted a full-scale search. We dismounted and walked our tired ponies along with them, and Toby and Felix explained about Patchy's shoe. Then Daddy wanted to know about Mr. Carter and when I got to the bit about his battered face and hands and how they looked much more as though he'd been fighting than falling from walls, Daddy said that surface injuries were often very deceptive, especially bruising, and it was sometimes very difficult to tell if people's stories were true even with a full examination and X-ray, but he might hear something on the grapevine and if he did, he'd let me know.

SIX

I slept late and was awakened by the telephone, but Louisa had answered it and I heard her saying with great firmness that the ponies had spent the whole day searching for lost people and simply had to rest. As she embarked on the whole saga of Mr. Carter and Toby I dozed off again and presently she came rushing into my room to say that it was Carolyn and they had wanted us to go over right away as they had seen smoke rising from Menacoell. I said we couldn't possibly, so we fixed it for tomorrow. William was not at all pleased.

'The Jacksons might like some of their ponies exercised,' I suggested, sitting up.

'I never thought of that. But it would mean going without the Hamiltons and William wants as many boys as possible in case it comes to a fight.'

'Felix and Toby ride quite well,' I said thoughtfully. 'I'll ring Heather and see what she says.' I dressed quickly in jeans and went down, without washing, to telephone.

'Well, of course you can borrow any of them,' she said when I had explained about the Mitchells and Menacoell and the exhausted state of our ponies, 'but I don't know about Felix and Toby. Do you think they'd be sensible on youngsters and realise you can't gallop and jump?'

'Yes, if you told them.'

'Well Jane's coming over. She's got around Dad to let her try Crackers again. I suppose Toby could manage Drummer, and if Mick and I ride Strongbow and Speedwell that'll leave Silver Sand for Felix and Bellboy for you.'

I protested at being given the best pony of all, but Heather said, 'I'd like you to ride him and see how you think his schooling's come on. You haven't tried him since Christmas.' She began to sound more cheerful as she planned. 'Yes, it's a great idea. We'll get them all out and that'll please Dad.'

Then I telephoned the Hamiltons and got Toby who said that Charlie Cort was coming to shoe Patchy, but if he could persuade his mother to see about it he would love to ride Drummer and he went off to ask her. Presently he came back to say that it would be all right and that Huw was already saddling Biscuit and Felix was sorting out his bicycle so they'd all be at the Jacksons' in about fifteen minutes. Then I rang the Mitchells to say that we were all coming after all.

Mummy was shopping in Baybourne so we left her a note explaining about Menacoell and the Jackson ponies needing exercise. Louisa made us some lunch while I ate breakfast, and then after a quick visit to Redwing, we set off up the road. We banged on Jane's door as we passed, but no one answered so we guessed she'd gone early and was helping to groom.

'She's the only person I've ever met who really *loves* grooming,' observed Louisa.

'When she's married she'll have a tremendously polished house like Mrs. Mitchell. But I do hope she's going to control Crackers today, we don't want her leading a runaway of all those young ponies.'

'If I'm having Dickon I'll ride next to you and then you can grab him if anything goes wrong. Though he's so small I'd never stop him if he really bolted off, because he doesn't understand a single aid yet.'

We were the last to arrive. Mick announced that all the ponies were groomed and Heather was handing out spongey bath mats, in revoltingly sickly shades, and explaining that Dad had bought the trekking saddles so cheap down the market that none of them fitted. The bridles took some sorting out too. Normally Heather and Mick used their own bridles on anything they ride, but we were using nosebandless trekking bridles which were worn over head-collars, except for Crackers and Silver Sand, who were to have the proper bridles with dropped nosebands.

We set off in a very orderly cavalcade. I was made the leader and when I looked back at them, all so young and unpredictable, I rather shivered in my shoes. If anything went wrong I was going to have to grab half-a-dozen uncontrollable ponies. I looked forward to the moment when William and Carolyn would join us.

We could only walk and trot which had a sobering effect on Silver Sand and Crackers. And Pirate, who had been put between Crackers and Drummer, seemed intimidated by their size and didn't attack either of them. Louisa was right at the back but Dickon seemed happy to follow the elderly and sensible Biscuit and I could hear Huw chattering away, so I assumed they were all right. Feeling as though I were a harassed instructor in charge of a large party of incompetent trekkers, I led my crocodile slowly across Middle Moor. We didn't have to go all the way to Chilmarth because William and Carolyn suddenly appeared, riding to meet us. They seemed very pleased that we had come, and inspected all our unusual mounts with interest. William was very scathing over poor Drummer and said that he had the smallest and weakest hocks he'd ever seen, but he approved of Speedwell and Strongbow. I felt much happier with these reliable reinforcements and became quite light-hearted as we swung left and crossed the Baybourne-Redbridge road to North Moor.

William said that he hadn't had to have a single filling and the dentist had said his teeth were first class. Then he told me his father was giving him a shotgun as a reward for doing so well in his mock exams and that they were going skiing in one of the best places in Switzerland next Christmas. As you can tell, William is one of those people who seem so successful that ten minutes in their company makes you feel cast-down and inferior and generally dissatisfied with your own life and puny efforts.

The first part of this way up Menacoell is a wide grassy track and Heather said it was a perfect place to give the young ponies their first canters as the hill would stop them and we wouldn't have to pull at their mouths. We arranged ourselves in parties. Zephyr, who won't wait without becoming hysterical, was to go first, followed by Speedwell and Strongbow, then William followed by Crackers and Silver Sand and Pirate. Then me with Drummer and Dickon and Biscuit. The first lot seemed to behave beautifully, but the second party went off at breakneck speed and Crackers and Silver Sand were past William in a flash and racing away up the track as though in the Derby. As they vanished from sight we could hear Jane storming, 'Whoa, Crackers, Whoa! You awful pony. Will you stop this minute!' Pirate seemed to be behaving himself and made no attempt to savage Brutus's ample behind.

Then we set off. I said that Huw could go ahead of me and as fast as he liked, because I didn't think Biscuit could go all that fast. Drummer and Dickon were to follow me and at first I looked back, worrying lest they might buck, but what with riders to carry and the uphill slope it seemed to be all they could do to keep going.

When we reached the others we found that Jane had fallen off. Carolyn and the Jacksons had blocked the path with their ponies, Crackers had to stop suddenly and Jane had landed heavily on her nose. The nose looked rather large and red, but we decided that it wasn't broken as it looked straight. (Louisa said it *could* be broken and stay straight but if so you didn't need to do much about it, it mended itself.) Then we inspected Jane for shock, but she seemed scarlet from shame and not the least bit pale, so we decided that there couldn't be much wrong with her and rode on.

We began to plan the assault on Menacoell. William, who was spoiling for a fight, said that the boys must make a surprise attack, charging in a body and overwhelming the trespassers. Toby and Huw thought this a great idea, but Felix pointed out that we didn't know whom the trespassers were yet and if we rushed in on some witch-like old lady and gave her a heart attack we'd feel very silly. Toby said Felix was nervous as usual and William said witch-like old ladies don't smoke and Heather said of course they did. Mick said we had no reason to think the trespassers were the same as the last lot and Felix said we needed information and should send in spies. I pointed out that the spies had better be dismounted because of neighing, and creeping being easier without a pony.

Mick suggested that we divided into two parties and approached the cottage from opposite sides. William said all right, but he wanted another good fighter in his party as Carolyn was hopeless. So we gave him Toby, who said he was a great fighter and was already flexing his muscles in a warlike manner, and Huw, whose eyes were shining at the prospect of battle, and Jane because we wanted to get her away from the more excitable of the young ponies. Then we agreed to meet again on the same spot the moment our spies returned.

Just as everything was settled Pirate suddenly flew at Dickon, and the little grey, who had more fight in him than Biscuit, gave an angry squeal and lashed out, landing several good kicks. Pirate promptly said that all his legs were broken and stood trembling with the shock of being stood up to. We couldn't see much wrong besides a few cuts and some swellings coming up in non-vital places, so we told him it was his own fault and set off in our two parties.

As we came near to the cottage we kept silent. There wasn't a great deal of cover. In the summer we could have found a patch of bracken, but now there was only a broken-down stone wall behind which to lurk. William's party were better off as they had all the sheep pens on their side of the cottage.

We lurked behind our wall and as everyone but Tracy wanted to be a spy we drew lots with blades of grass and Heather and Felix drew the longest. They decided that they would creep along the rocky hillside above the flat shelf of land and look down on the cottage. They crept off and Mick and I were left holding their ponies. Holding ponies is one of the most boring occupations I know, especially when they are fidgets like Silver Sand. He always wanted to eat the piece of grass on which I was standing and if I took my eye off him for a moment he had a foot through his reins. But at least it was a fine day with hazy sunshine warming our backs and Mick, Louisa and I were able to talk in low voices while we waited. Poor Tracy sat apart like a leper with Pirate.

It seemed ages before we saw our spies returning, slipping back from boulder to boulder in quite a spy-like manner.

'Looks as though there's people there then.' Mick sounded quite excited. 'They wouldn't creep about if it was empty.'

'We saw four of them,' said Felix, joining us behind the wall. 'All youngish men.'

'Hippy types.' Heather seemed disapproving. 'Two with beards, all with long hair, tatty, dirty, long hair; they need Dawn re-styling them.'

'At least four of them,' Felix went on gloomily, 'and all six-footers.'

'Well, they weren't dwarfs,' qualified Heather.

'I wouldn't like to risk a direct confrontation,' said Felix. 'We could come off very much the worse. We'll have to use cunning.'

We had mounted and were just moving off down hill to the meeting place when we heard a loud, urgent neigh, a thunder of hoofs and a familiar voice shouting, 'Whoa, Crackers, whoa!' Heather groaned and we all stood in our stirrups, risking discovery to see what was going on. We realised that Crackers, finding himself without his favourite Jackson ponies, had come in search of them, straight through the sheep pens, past the back door of the cottage and was now cantering purposefully at a large well-preserved wall. He sailed into the air with a terrific spring that shot Jane out of the saddle. Stiff and straight she nose-dived to the ground. We had all dismounted and were endeavouring to keep ourselves and ponies down behind the wall, as we waited for the noisy, neighing Crackers to give us away. Louisa grabbed his rein as he plunged among us, greeting his friends with the enthusiasm of the long lost horse, touching noses and whinneying.

'You big stupid,' Heather muttered at him. Mick was peering over the wall. 'They've got her. There's five of them around her. She's getting up: she's on her feet, I think she's all right.'

'I wonder what sort of story she's telling them,'

said Felix. 'Look, hadn't someone better be her friend looking for her and take Crackers back? A girl, they'll be less suspicious of girls.'

'You go Frances; you'll be much the best at backing up whatever story Jane's told, and you'll be able to escape easily on Bellboy if they try to keep you.' I couldn't argue with Heather. I *was* riding the only reliable pony in our party. So I mounted and took Crackers from Louisa. I waited until the others had vanished down the track to the rendezvous and then I began to call, 'Jane, Jane!' in my most feminine voice. I had decided to appear as a thoroughly silly character with a grasshopper mind, partly to lull them into a comfortable security and partly so that if Jane and I told different stories they'd just think I was a bit dotty.

'Jane, where are you?' I called, leading Crackers over a low place in our crumbling wall and heading for the cottage. '*Jane!* Are you all right?' I injected a very anxious note into my voice as I trotted towards the group by the large wall. The young men were mostly dressed in jeans and Afghanistan sheepskin coats. They had, as Heather said, horrid hair, and three of them were pale and spotty. The other two had black eyes and swollen faces and looked as though they had been fighting.

Jane said, 'Yes, I'm O.K. now. We've found my glasses. But I can't stop Crackers, it's no use I just can't. He bolted off with me and jumped wall after wall before this huge one.' Jane's face was scarlet with misery and she looked as though she was about to burst into tears of despair.

'Well, you ride Bellboy,' I said, dismounting quickly

and climbing aboard Crackers with equal speed just in case a quick getaway became necessary. Jane was arguing, 'I'll ruin him, Heather will never forgive me.'

'Heather won't know,' I said, giving her a fierce look. I didn't want her giving away how many more of us were lurking.

As Jane hopped round trying to mount Bellboy with my too short stirrup one of the young men asked, 'Are you locals?'

'Yes,' I pointed vaguely, 'we live over the other side of the moor.'

'Do the ponies belong to you?'

'No, to Mr. Jackson. He runs the trekking centre.' Jane was fiddling with her stirrups. I decided to collect information. 'You don't belong to these parts?'

'No, we're just camping, and finding an empty cottage, well there's no sense in freezing in a tent when you don't have to, so we moved in.'

'Well you'd better not leave a mess or you'll have Mr. Mitchell after you. He's very fussy about litter.'

'You mean the place is used?'

'Oh yes, it's the shepherd's cottage. When the sheep come up on the moor someone has to look after them. They'll be up next week, I expect,' I added, hoping to hurry them out of our cottage.

'And where does this Mitchell bloke hang out?'

'At the big farm down on the road.' I pointed. Jane was mounted at last. I took a look round the pale faces, the fair beards, the black eyes. I knew I'd never remember them clearly.

'Come on,' I told Jane, 'we must hurry.'

Jane said goodbye to the young men and I swept

away on the eager Crackers. At the far end of the terrace I stopped and looked back. They were watching us and one of them had a pair of binoculars.

Jane was patting Bellboy. 'Oh, he's lovely. So smooth and easy to pull up. But why were you in such a hurry?' she asked as she followed me downhill. 'They seemed quite a friendly lot, but you were so standoffish, just like William.'

'We don't want them there, it's *our* camping place.'

'I call that selfish.'

I concentrated on controlling Crackers who was in two minds about galloping flat out down Menacoell. I couldn't really explain my feelings of hostility when I didn't understand them myself.

The others seemed very relieved to see us. But I could see that Heather was looking from me to Jane. 'We changed over, I hope you don't mind. She simply can't control Crackers.'

'Never mind about the ponies,' said William. 'What were the trespassers like? Did you speak to them?'

I repeated my conversation and then Jane burst in rather indignantly. 'There's nothing wrong with them. They helped me find my glasses. I was getting quite friendly with them when Frances came over and was so sharp and snooty.'

'I should have been sharp too,' said William, 'but now they know the cottage belongs to someone they may move out.'

'They may squat and try to become self-sufficient,' observed Felix. 'You could grow beans, keep chickens and goats.'

'Let's go and have lunch by the stream,' suggested Heather. 'My stomach's rattling.'

As we ate we discussed ways and means of evicting the trespassers without force. William's plan was to turn the water supply bright green. Mick thought a flock of baaing sheep on the doorstep would probably do the trick. I favoured haunting them every night in the characters of the local ghosts. Toby suggested stink bombs and Felix thought spreading a rumour that the last occupant of the cottage had died of plague or leprosy would soon drive them out. Louisa said that it was stupid to use diseases which everyone knew had been stamped out in England, but if they heard that there had been trouble with the drains and the water getting mixed up and people had had typhoid they might believe it. Heather pointed out that it was difficult to get a rumour to people who lived so far from anyone else and we'd have to find where they bought their baked beans and coke.

In the end we decided that the water supply being cut off or a flock of sheep with us in charge would be the best methods, but both of those needed Mr. Mitchell's agreement before they could be put into action and William and Carolyn said they would talk it over with him that night. Everyone but Jane agreed that something must be done quickly. It was bad enough losing Menacoell for these holidays, but it would be an absolute disaster if we couldn't camp there in the summer.

SEVEN

Our day on Menacoell ended with another, quite different sort of disaster. It was only after we had parted from the Mitchells that I realised Heather had become unusually silent and subdued and I began to wonder whether I had offended her by letting Jane go on riding Bellboy. But surely, I thought, she must see that it was working very well? Jane rode a hundred times better on a schooled pony. She just wasn't experienced enough for green and wild ones. And I was enjoying myself on Crackers, I liked his excitement and enthusiasm, and I'd learned that he was quite easy to control provided you were ready to say 'no' the moment he thought up some hare-brained reason for a flat-out gallop.

We had a peaceful ride home. The young ponies, striding along, ears pricked, looked much older and more sophisticated than when they had set out; they seemed pleased with themselves and proud to be carrying riders.

As we came up the lane to Black Tor I saw Mr. Jackson hurry to the gate and then he stood watching us ride into the yard.

'Well, that's better and no mistake,' he said in a pleased voice. 'You've certainly settled that lot down.' I could see he was visualising a great cavalcade of profitable trekkers. He looked from me to Jane. 'You couldn't manage Crackers then?'

'No, I'm not good enough. I admit defeat. He behaves perfectly with Frances but he just bolts off with me. Now Bellboy's a saint,' she patted him, 'good and obliging and so well schooled.'

'Why don't you have him then?' asked Mr. Jackson. 'He's a bit more expensive, but it's worth it if he suits you.'

'Have Bellboy?' Jane sounded horrified. 'But he's Heather's. He's Heather's own pony.'

'Well, we've plenty more; she can take her pick: Speedwell, Strongbow, Crackers . . .'

'But she's trained Bellboy and made him perfect. You can't just sell him, she loves him,' objected Jane, looking wildly round for support. Heather had vanished into the stable and suddenly I realised why she had been cast down all the way home. She had foreseen that this would happen and it was all my fault. I had to speak for her. I knew that to Mr. Jackson talk of loving ponies was just being sentimental, so I tried another tack.

'Heather's put so much work into him, you must let her ride him in the hunter trials and the show,' I protested. 'It wouldn't be fair to take him away now. However hard she works on the others they won't be ready for competitions this year.'

'I daresay Jane will let her have him back for the odd class,' said Mr. Jackson. 'It's a business with us, you see. We can't hang on to the good 'uns and sell the bad 'uns. We wouldn't have any customers.'

'I couldn't do it, I really couldn't,' said Jane. 'Not for anything.'

'Up to you,' said Mr. Jackson, and went off towards the house.

Heather had retreated to the darkest corner of the stable and was unsaddling Speedwell. She didn't say anything so we all guessed she might be crying and stood about feeling awful and wondering what to do with the ponies. At last Mick realised what had happened and took charge.

Felix and Toby walked home with Louisa and me, at least Felix walked, pushing his bicycle, while Toby rode his in slow and perilous serpentines which narrowly missed our toes.

'It's awful for Heather,' he said. 'I'd go mad if Dad announced that he was selling Patchy, all coolly like that.'

'I suppose she'll need a bigger one soon,' Felix seemed to be looking for a bright side, 'but it would be far better if poor Tracy could have Bellboy; that Pirate's a really foul pony. I had to give up Patchy to Toby and eventually I'll have to hand over Minstrel and Huw'll get Patchy, but it's nothing like so bad when it's all in the family.'

'Except for the one who takes over. You never stopped telling me how to ride Patchy for the first six months.'

'I was more experienced on him and most people like advice from the previous owner.'

'Not rammed down their throats, they don't.'

I was too upset by my part in this new disaster to have much patience with the Hamiltons. 'Oh, do shut up!' I said. 'I've never known people go on and on about boring old quarrels like you two do. Why don't you try to think of some way of helping Heather?'

I was still trying to work out a way of helping Heather next morning when we heard the sound of hoofs scrunching on the gravel. Mummy and Louisa and I all said, 'Jane!' and then groaned that she never seemed to idle or lie in bed even on a Sunday. But when we looked out it wasn't Jane, it was Heather. This was a surprise, because the Jacksons don't normally make social calls, but I rushed out and invited Bellboy into a box and Heather into elevenses.

We were cooking. As it looked as though the whole family were to be in to a meal for once, Mummy had decided on a slap-up lunch and made a very special and delicious ice cream. Louisa had offered to do the Yorkshire pudding and, not to look lazy, I'd said I'd organise the vegetables. So Mummy put the joint in, remarked how nice it was to have daughters of a sensible age, and went off to read the Sunday papers. We provided Heather with chocolate biscuits and bitter lemon and got on with our whisking and pan-boiling. She took a very long time to come to the point. We discussed Brutus and his hoofs; he still winced like an elderly gentleman every time he trod on a sharp stone. 'Dad says he's got dropped soles and they never do on the moor,' Heather told us. Then we got on to the Hamiltons and Mummy came in to beat up her ice cream in the middle of our discussion on their quarrelling.

'If I were their mother I'd send them to different schools and persuade them to develop different skills so there were areas where they *couldn't* compete. Of course their father is very successful,' she added, as she stuffed the ice cream back into the freezer, 'that may have something to do with it. He may make them feel they've got to be brilliant to earn his love, and that can be disastrous, especially with boys.'

'Perhaps it's not all that much better having rich parents then,' observed Heather and came at last to the point. 'I want you to speak to Jane, Frances. Tell her it's all right for her to have Bellboy. I tried to talk to them this morning but they were going to church. Mrs. Shaw says she doesn't mind paying the extra, but she won't take my pony from me. I tried to explain that Dad's right really. We're not rich and it's no use behaving as if we were. The ponies are a business and we get a lot of fun out of them, but they've got to be sold once they're trained just as the sheep and cattle have to go to the butcher. So if you could speak to Mrs. Shaw and explain that Bellboy's bound to be sold soon and I'd much rather he went to Jane, who'd really love him and look after him, than an unknown person. And if he isn't sold Dad's sure to take him for the trekkers, and you know what they're like.'

We looked at her sadly, 'Well, if you're sure that's what you really want —'

'Yes, I've decided. And Dad says now that Mick and I really put some value on the ponies he'll give us a rake off on the ones we've schooled, so I'm going to save all my money and one day I'll buy a horse that's really my own and ride at Badminton.' As she said

this Heather drank the rest of her bitter lemon in a very
determined manner and then said she must go.

I went out to help her saddle Bellboy and I promised
that I would see the Shaws that afternoon, but I did it
with a heavy heart for Heather was avoiding my eyes
and I knew that she didn't want me to see how unhappy
she felt at this parting with Bellboy.

Daddy did get a call from a patient, just as we sat
down to our delicious lunch, but luckily it wasn't all
that urgent and could wait until three o'clock. So we
talked and ate and admired each other's cooking and
then, when we'd washed up, I set off for the Shaws'.
Louisa refused to come with me. She said that *she*
hadn't promised Heather. I didn't really mind; sometimes it's easier to have a serious talk if there are no
members of your family present.

The Shaws wanted me to eat and drink, but they let
me off when I explained about our lunch. I quickly
brought the conversation to the reason for my visit and
told them that since Bellboy had to earn his keep or be
sold, Heather would much rather that Jane, who loved
ponies and was super at stable management, had him
than a total stranger, and the alternative was to watch
him being slowly wrecked by trekkers.

'But I'm no good either, not at the actual thing,'
said Jane sadly. 'I shall wreck him.'

'You're streets better than the trekkers. Some of
them have never been on a horse before and Mr.
Jackson won't agree to Mick and Heather giving them
proper lessons first. He thinks they'll learn as they go
along, but most of them don't. They sit like lumps at
the back of the saddle and when they trot they heave

themselves up by the reins. Some ponies don't seem to mind. Trudy, Misty, the Drummer-type — they just like a quiet life. But Bellboy's far too good for it. The trekkers would drive him mad.'

'Poor Heather, what a choice!' said Mrs. Shaw. 'You think we should buy him, then?'

'Yes, it's the lesser evil, and when she gets over parting with him she'll be pleased.'

'I'll let her ride whenever she likes and I'll ask her to give me some lessons on him,' decided Jane.

I explained about the pony club hunter trials at the end of the month and how Heather had been schooling for them all through the year. Jane was very nice. She said that she would only buy him on condition that Heather agreed to ride him at the hunter trials, as she was sure she wouldn't do him justice.

When we had settled all that, they took me to see the little outhouse at the bottom of the garden which they were converting into a stable. Misty wasn't there because one of the Jackson relations had provided her with a field.

As I came out of number three Chapel Cottages there was P.C. Weston going into number four. He was in ordinary clothes and I remembered that one of the oldest inhabitants, Mrs. Black, was his granny. I asked after Mr. Carter.

'They put a few stitches in his head, but he's coming along nicely. I hear you had to go out again for one of the Hamilton boys.'

'Yes, and Barley Bog Plantation at dead of night is no joke.'

'You've only got the Moaning Pedlar there. Now at

Tolkenny, well, you name them, it's got them: white hares, grey ladies, headless horsemen, the lot.' He laughed, but being a local person he half believed in them.

Thinking of Mr. Carter was causing a sort of coming together of ideas at the back of my head. 'You've heard about those blokes up at Menacoell?' I asked.

'Yes, it's all around and Mr. Mitchell made a formal inquiry.'

'Well, two of them had been fighting and their bruises looked just about the same age as Mr. Carter's.'

P.C. Weston looked at me sharply. 'Did they now,' he said, 'and why shouldn't they have been fighting each other?'

'They seemed quite friendly, at least they didn't give each other looks of hate.'

'And Mr. Carter didn't say anything about a fight?'

'Not to us. He pretended he'd fallen off the wall, but he wasn't in the right place. I thought he might have told the police what really happened.'

'He could have crawled before he collapsed. But anyway I shall be making some inquiries about the lads up at Menacoell. They could be up to something, and with meat the price it is, sheep are well worth stealing, so I'll be glad if the local riders keep their eyes open for anything suspicious.'

'We'll do that,' I said, pleased with an official request to do just what I had intended.

'Well, that's what P.C. Weston said,' I told William when I rang Chilmarth on Monday morning.

'I agree about keeping an eye on them. I think we

should go up today. For one thing it's just possible that
they were only weekend campers, and if they've packed
and gone, we don't want to get stewed up over nothing.
My father's seeing his solicitor, but apparently possesion
is nine-tenths of the law.'

'You mean they'll stay for the whole summer and
ruin next holidays?' I asked dismally.

'Oh, don't be so gloomy, surely we can camp
somewhere else? Anyway, you and Louisa come over
this afternoon. Four's plenty if we're only going to
keep watch.'

We knew all the others were busy. Mrs. Shaw had
bought Bellboy on Sunday evening and Heather was to
give Jane her first lesson on him, and when Louisa and
Toby had met, going to post letters, he'd told her that
their father was making them help clear the overgrown
garden and they couldn't ride till Tuesday when he was
going back to London. 'Toby says his father believes
in child labour,' Louisa had reported in shocked tones.
'He says working in the mills would be a lot better for
us than watching television.'

'I expect he was exasperated with them,' Mummy
told her. 'Probably they'd spent the whole morning
quarrelling.'

We had a lovely ride with the Mitchells. Being only
four people on sensible ponies we were able to gallop
when and where we felt like it, without any looking
back over our shoulders. When we reached Menacoell
it appeared deserted. No smoke rose from the chimney
and no sound came from the cottage. My heart rose at
the thought that the hippies had gone and it was ours

again. William and I approached cautiously and peered
in through the windows. There was no one there, but
they seemed to have left their gear. We went in, feeling
stupidly like intruders though it was our house. There
were sleeping bags in every room and clothes thrown
everywhere. There were dirty plates left over from
breakfast, greasy frying pans, half-eaten tins of baked
beans and a few blackened sausages. We went out
again, away from the squalor and the smell of sleeping
bags, and told the others what we had found.

'My father's solicitor thinks that moving the shepherd
and the sheep up here would be the best bet,' said
William, when we paused from lamenting the occu-
pation. 'Cottages for stockmen are about the only ones
that really belong to landlords nowadays. I offered to
be the shepherd since Jim Turner wouldn't think of
living up here.'

'If they were poor homeless families it would be
different,' observed Louisa. 'I wouldn't mind giving it
up to someone who really needed somewhere to live,
because we only use it occasionally.'

'No, these are just middle class squatters,' said
William. 'My father's solicitor says it's more a way of
life than a need.'

Then, since there seemed to be nothing we could do,
we went to Croft Lanvet and jumped the cross-country
course, and then we went back to Chilmarth and had
tea. It was a very substantial tea of scones and clotted
cream and home-made jam and cake and we ate it in
the Mitchell's highly polished dining-room which shows
up every crumb and the worst of it is that the dogs

aren't allowed in, so there's no one to hoover them up.

Afterwards Louisa and I rode home sedately, for we were feeling very full and rather bloated.

As we came to St. Dinas we saw a police car waiting on the road and P.C. Weston leaning against it and watching our approach. We broke into a trot wondering if he had interesting or exciting news for us, though, as Louisa said, the last thing we wanted was to be sent off in another search party.

'I thought it was you coming,' he said, 'so I stopped by to tell you about these lads up at Menacoell. It seems they're here to make a film. They're employed by a small company that makes 'shorts' and documentaries and they've been sent to get acclimatised. London's checked up on their office for us and says they're all above board, so I reckon we can stop worrying about the sheep.'

I felt curiously disappointed at this explanation. But P.C. Weston looked pleased and Louisa said, 'Well, that's a relief.' I tried to feel pleased too. After all it *is* much better to have a film company in your neighbourhood than a gang of characters you suspect of being crooks. But somehow I couldn't feel pleased; I felt decidedly let down.

The result of our meeting with P.C. Weston was that when William telephoned after supper, full of the news that the young men belonged to a film company which wanted to use Menacoell in a film about smugglers, he was disappointed that I wasn't more overwhelmed. But I agreed that it was absolutely super that they only wanted Menacoell for a week at the outside and had promised to leave it clean and tidy when they left.

When, later still, Heather telephoned it was a bit more exciting. She said that the film company had asked Dad to supply pack ponies for the smugglers. They thought it would only be for two days and they were dropping in the pack saddles in the morning so that the ponies could get used to them. Then she asked if Louisa and I would help because with twelve ponies to train and deliver to Pennecford, they were going to need some help. I asked why they were going to Pennecford and she said that the smugglers had to meet a boat and so one was coming up the estuary, but it was all very complicated because of the times of the tides.

I said we'd love to help and was she asking the Hamiltons and the Mitchells and Jane? Heather said definitely Jane, probably the Hamiltons, but she thought the Mitchells were a bit too grand. I agreed they wouldn't want to help with the training, but I said I would tell them about the filming as they might like to watch. Then we arranged that Louisa and I would go over after lunch next day.

As we walked up the lane to Black Tor Farm a large, dark blue van on its way out, squeezed us against the wall. It had Image Films Ltd boldly printed on its side so we guessed that it had just delivered the saddles. We found all the Jacksons and Hamiltons gathered around inspecting the twelve large, rather dirty felt and leather pack saddles. They had a wooden framework that made an X front and back, a lot of metal Ds and a complicated arrangement of straps. Heather said the little ponies would be lost in them and Toby sniffed and observed that he bet they'd been used on camels last.

Mr. Jackson began to tell us about the old days. 'They used to use no end of pack ponies in these parts. There weren't any roads to speak of, you see, so it was the old sledge or the pack pony. They didn't have any need of wheels. They called the pack saddles Crooks and they used to carry hay, manure, bricks, any mortal thing. My old grandfather remembered it well.'

We moved on to inspect the twenty-four basket panniers, large and tall. They were to hang on either side of the saddles. I didn't think the ponies would like them much.

'I think smugglers strapped the kegs of brandy straight on the saddles,' said Felix. 'I don't think they used these pannier things. I'm sure I've seen pictures.'

'Well, this is how Mr. Coombes wants it, so we've got to get the ponies quiet-like,' said Mr. Jackson, 'and don't anyone forget and try to go through the stable door or a narrow gate with that lot on!' He laughed and went off towards the house saying he'd leave us to it.

'We've rounded up *all* the ponies, except the mares that have got foals or are about to have them,' explained Heather. 'That roan thing is Kismet. She's supposed to be in foal, but Dad says she's barren again so we're going to use her. The one with the awful knees is Taffy. He broke them so badly the vet didn't think he'd be much good, but he seems pretty sound now. And that skinny thing Jane's grooming is Juniper. Dad bought him down the market and he's picked up a bit, but we didn't want to use him till the summer.'

Still, as Mr. Coombes said, you don't see much pony once you've got those panniers on,' observed

Mick. 'And he doesn't want pulled manes, Jane, or plaits, the smugglers never bothered!' Jane stood up for herself. 'Even smugglers would have taken out last year's burrs,' she said, unravelling Juniper's tail.

Heather said we must work in pairs, one to hold the pony and the other to fix the panniers, and she seemed to have worked out in advance who was to go with whom. She had Louisa, Mick had Toby, Felix and I were together and Jane was allowed to go on with her grooming. Huw and Tracy had scoops of oats for rewards and were to help anyone who needed them. We started on the easy ponies: Trudy, Misty and Gipsy. We put bridles on them, so that they couldn't drag us around if they became unnerved, and then the pack saddles. None of them seemed to notice anything unusual, not even, as Toby put it, the smell of camel. But, when we produced the panniers they eyed them doubtfully and we made them all have a really good look before we lifted them on to their backs. The two baskets were strapped together and fitted neatly over the saddles, then there were more straps to buckle on the various Ds. It seemed quite an efficient arrangement to me, but Felix still said they were wrong for smugglers.

Our pony was Misty and when she was over the first shock of her burden, we took her off for a graze. Then we pushed the baskets about to make sure that she wasn't frightened by the feel of them against her sides, and finally we loaded them with logs of wood and half empty sacks and bags from the barn. Then we made all three ponies look at each other, which they did with slightly raised eyebrows. Then we unloaded

and took the panniers off and put them on again and
reloaded, and as none of the ponies took any notice at
all this time, Heather said they were trained and we
could start on the next three.

Felix and I swopped Misty for Crackers whose eyes
goggled and goggled at the sight of the panniers. We
put hay in them and offered him oats from them and
gradually he seemed slightly less horrified. We showed
him Silver Sand and Mousie wearing theirs and his
eyes nearly goggled out of their sockets, so I wore
them across my shoulders and then Felix cantered about
in them pretending to be a horse, while Crackers looked
on in amazement. Finally we sent for reinforcements
and Heather came and helped me lift the panniers on
very gently while Felix talked calmingly and Tracy fed
handfuls of oats. Then we led him up and down the
lane and for a long time he rushed nervously, as though
by hurrying he could leave these monsters behind, but
eventually he calmed down and began to graze in a
relaxed manner.

Crackers had taken so long that Mick and Heather
were already on their third pupils – Drummer and
Poppy. We took Tinker, the little, old, grey-muzzled
pony who had taught Tracy to ride and now, no longer
up to fast work, was kept for small children. She didn't
mind the panniers at all but she looked rather pathetic
and over-burdened by their hugeness. We pointed this
out to Heather, who said we wouldn't use her unless
we had to; if Juniper and Taffy were up to it and
Kismet and Pirate behaved, we had twelve without
her, or the three nervous young ponies, but we did
need a spare ready trained. Pirate was our last pupil.

He also was dwarfed by the panniers, but being young and strong he didn't look pathetic. He didn't seem at all nervous and, after biting me once, as I pulled up his girth, and getting a sharp slap in retaliation, he behaved beautifully.

Kismet, calm, fat and ponderous, looked in foal to me, but Heather said that Dad swore she wasn't and he usually knew. Taffy's knees were unsightly, but he seemed sound and Mick said a bit of boot polish would work wonders with the scars. Juniper, a well-bred chestnut, was ribby, but he didn't look shockingly thin, so it was agreed that all three of them should be shod when Charlie Cort came that evening. Then Heather counted out bridles and made us arrange sets of tack round the barn ready for the next day's filming. We were to meet the Image people in the Croft Lanvet lane at six and they were to lead the ponies to Pennecford and then, when the boat was unloaded, up to Menacoell. It would probably be dark by the time we took over again to lead them home. We agreed to take torches and as much to eat as we could carry and Jane said she supposed it would all be off if it rained? But Heather said Mr. Coombes wanted us whatever the weather. He'd said a thunderstorm would make it all the more dramatic, and they would shoot both evenings and combine the best shots.

EIGHT

Getting off on Wednesday evening was a nightmare. With nine riding ponies and twelve pack ponies the yard at Black Tor was crammed to the brim. We soon found it was almost impossible to get the panniers on by yourself, especially if you were holding another pony, and everyone began to panic that we would be late.

Mr. Jackson was supposed to be helping us, but he would keep counting the ponies and coming up with a different number every time. He wouldn't believe that Heather had the whole thing worked out, and it wasn't until Mick told him to go and look in the barn and see if there were any packs left over that he finally calmed down and became useful. Tracy and Huw were marvellous; they had tied Dickon and Biscuit up and were rushing round helping everyone, heaving on panniers, holding down excited ponies, shooing on reluctant ones.

At last we were all mounted. I had been given Crackers and Pirate to lead and complained of this injustice, but Heather pointed out that I had Redwing while she and Mick were riding the newly broken ponies, and Jane wasn't used to riding and leading so they'd only given her Misty. Felix and Toby each had two sensible ones. Louisa only had Poppy so she offered to swop her for one of mine if they were both tiresome.

I led the cavalcade of twenty-one ponies down the lane and it sounded as though an army were scrunching and clattering behind me. Redwing, though squashed by panniers at intervals, obviously felt that she was in a position of some importance and behaved beautifully. Crackers jogged excitedly. Pirate looked as though butter wouldn't melt in his mouth and didn't even roll his eyes. All seemed to be going well. But we had only ridden a little way in to Middle Moor when there was a cry from behind, Mick was in trouble. Strongbow had been squashed between his two led horses on the narrow path and was now petrified of their panniers and refusing to go forward at all. Louisa offered to take one of his ponies, but Mick decided that he would change the saddles and ride Silver Sand, only then, as Strongbow couldn't be expected to carry panniers, some other pony had to take two pairs. We settled on Trudy, whose back is endless, but the reorganisation seemed to take hours and Heather was becoming frantic. We set off again and I refused to hurry, because the led ponies were already tumbling and slipping on the rough going they were compelled to take. The path was never wide enough for three abreast. So Heather fumed and Felix did his best to calm her by pointing out that film companies were always behind in their schedules and it wasn't as though we were keeping some grand and expensive star waiting. Actually we reached the

Croft Lanvet lane only three-and-a-half minutes late by
the average time of all our watches and there was no
sign of Mr. Marty Coombes and Image Films Ltd.

We waited, letting the ponies graze because we didn't
think smugglers would care about dirty bits. Mick
changed his saddle back to Strongbow and then, just as
we were beginning to think they had forgotten or
changed their minds, a motorcade of dark blue vehicles
came in sight. One of them was a minibus and it
disgorged a group of villainous-looking characters
wearing knee breeches, stockings and buckled shoes.
Some had tattered frock coats and the others just loose
shirts and enormous belts stuck full of weapons. They
had all tied their long hair back and one or two wore
coloured handkerchiefs round their heads. Behind them
came a short tubby man in a shiny suit, a tall blonde
woman with huge dark glasses and a good-looking
man of about forty in a well-cut grey suit. He had
noticeably blue eyes and when he spoke it was with an
American accent.

Heather and Mick said, 'Good evening, Mr.
Coombes,' in their best trekking stable manner.
Heather explained that most of the ponies were dead
easy but that one or two needed handling and asked if
any of the smugglers had any experience, but they all
said no and made stupid jokes. Mr. Coombes didn't
seem to have much idea of organising things, so we
each took over the nearest smuggler and explained
how to lead ponies. I got a red-headed one with a huge
beard called Ginge. He looked rather silly with Crackers
in one hand and Pirate in the other. They were such
different sizes. So I suggested to Mr. Coombes, whom

everyone called Marty and who addressed all males as 'Pardner' and all females as either 'Honey' or 'Sweetie', that we changed Pirate round. In the end we gave him and Poppy to the smallest smuggler of all who was called Kev, and we gave Ginge Silver Sand as a pair for Crackers. As Felix said, they were both goers and would at least tow him in the same direction.

At last they were sorted out and set off up the road but, unluckily, the smuggler with the black patch over his eye, who was leading Trudy and Misty, had taken the lead so the cavalcade moved at funereal speed. It was lovely to be rid of led ponies and panniers. We could all ride together and talk.

Felix seemed dissatisfied. 'It all looks wrong. I'm sure pack ponies didn't go in pairs; they went in long strings, single file, a rope from the bridle of one tied to the pack of the next.'

The rest of us looked at the cavalcade doubtfully; we didn't know. 'The whole point of pack animals is that they go where there are no roads or when the roads are deep in mud and impassable for wheels. And the smugglers don't look right either, they're much more like pirates.'

'Felix Hamilton, the well-known film critic,' mocked Toby. 'I bet Marty Coombes knows more about it than you do. You haven't even seen the script. How do you know it's not adapted from a book which says exactly what everyone was wearing?'

'I'm entitled to have an opinion,' said Felix.

I didn't know whether Marty Coombes knew how to direct films, but it soon became plain he didn't understand ponies. With Trudy and Misty walking at two miles an hour Crackers and Silver Sand kept catching up with them and Trudy, who was in season, had begun to squeal and kick. At last Heather and I could stand it no longer so we agreed to go together and suggest action to Marty Coombes. The really big van, which Felix said probably carried the props, was behind us and the open Land-Rover with a camera mounted in the back led the whole troop, but Marty was in the minibus, between us and the pack ponies, so it was quite easy to trot alongside.

'Mr. Coombes,' began Heather and then nearly giggled when he said, 'Make it Marty, sweetie.' However, she recovered and, putting on her best trekking-centre voice, explained that he had the two slowest ponies in front, which was causing trouble and could we change them round.

'Anything you say, honey. You go ahead, you're the boss of the pony department.'

'You're not filming, yet then?' I asked. 'We don't want to mess things up.' Marty waved us on, so feeling rather bossy, we made Black Patch change places with Ginge and then we told Kev to slap Pirate who was making rude faces at Poppy.

It was very boring hacking along the road to Pennecford, instead of taking the short cut across the Chilmarth fields, but Heather said we had to stay with the pack ponies in case there was trouble. Presently there was a bit of activity and the Land-Rover darted about and seemed to be taking shots of the smugglers with the moor rising behind them. Felix said if they *were* shooting they were getting some nice shots of telegraph poles which wouldn't look too good in a period film.

The Mitchells had waved and shouted as we passed Chilmarth and now they came trotting down the road to join us. We told them our adventures so far, giggled over Marty Coombes, and began to eat our suppers. When we left the Baybourne-Redbridge road and took the narrow one beside the estuary, the journey became more interesting. It was almost high tide so the water stretched wide across the mudbanks. It had brimmed over the grass verge and was seeping gently across the road. The moored boats bobbed. I thought that they looked cheerful, glad to be free of the mud. The seagulls bobbed too. For the moment they looked like contented farmyard ducks.

We passed through St. Nechtan's: a single row of what were fishermen's cottages, until the pilchards moved elsewhere and the fishermen lost their livelihood. Now the cottages belonged to people who sailed, and, at weekends and in the summer, there were dinghies and boat trailers and cars parked everywhere. The bridle road across the Chilmarth land came out there, down a lane beside a tiny church, where the fishermen who died of old age or whose bodies were washed ashore were buried. Then we came to Pennecford itself, quite a big village, with three roads running uphill from the estuary. People heard the sound of hoofs and came out to see what was going on and stood to stare at the smugglers. They looked at the vans and, seeing Image Films Ltd, told each other that it was a film; no one came to ask questions of us. The tide was high now and the water was all over the road, lapping at the pavement in front of the ships' chandlers and the Mariners' Arms. I wondered how the smugglers' buckled shoes were faring. At the end the estuary deepens and quite decent-sized boats can come into Pennecford's little harbour at high tide. The quay does have an old-fashioned look and I thought the ancient Mariners' Arms looked very suitable for a smugglers' inn. But Felix was complaining that the plastic motor boats should be moored elsewhere and the string of fairy lights *must* be taken from the front of the pub.

William said, 'I expect it's just a short being made on a shoe-string budget; it costs a fortune to do things well.'

'It wouldn't take me ten minutes to take those lights down,' argued Felix.

'If you touched them they'd never work again. Look what happened when you took over the Christmas tree. And then the publican would sue the film company for new lights at vast expense,' said Toby.

'Perhaps the cameraman is only going to film the lower half,' suggested Carolyn, in an attempt to keep the peace.

Then the smugglers showed signs of excitement; they turned to watch a very odd-looking vessel that was coming up the river. It was a modern sailing boat but it had been provided with old-fashioned sails and rigging which flapped and sagged and billowed ineffectually, as it came steadily up river under its engine. It slowed as it came into the harbour and Marty addressed it through a loudhailer. Then the crew produced a sort of false bulwark that fitted over one side and combined with the sails to give that half of the boat a very old-fashioned appearance. But, knowing nothing about boats, I couldn't tell if it looked suitable for smugglers. The ponies were being lined up outside the Mariners'

Arms, which seemed to be going into the film, fairy lights and all.

Meanwhile the boat came in frontwards, looking very peculiar indeed, and then turned its false side to the jetty and moored. The crew, who wore pirate costumes, organised a gang plank. A bit of an argument started among the film company about who was to go aboard and who hold the ponies, but when that was settled they began to unload the cargo. As they came running down the gang plank, each carrying a small wooden keg on his shoulder, I thought they looked rather good.

'Now that's quite authentic, isn't it?' I asked Felix. 'I'm sure I've seen illustrations of smugglers looking just like that.' But he was fidgeting about in an irritable way and didn't seem to hear. Then he said, 'Would you mind holding Minstrel a minute?'

I thought he wanted to rush to the gents in the Mariners' Arms, but he didn't. He crept through the ponies, while the camera was trained on the smugglers coming down the plank with another instalment of barrels, went round behind a group of bystanders and then appeared to be taking a closer look at the Land-Rover camera. Presently he came back. He didn't say anything but he seemed satisfied, so I decided he was just a film enthusiast and had wanted to note the exact size or type or something of the camera. I turned my attention to Heather who was worrying over the ponies' loads. It looked as though they were going to carry three kegs a pannier and Heather and Mick were watching carefully to see that the loads were properly balanced. They said that carrying a lopsided load up

Menacoell would give any pony a sore back. I was wondering how heavy the kegs were empty and what they would have weighed full of brandy.

Our ponies were getting hungry and bored; they rubbed their bits against our backs, twirled round us and trod on our toes. Then they began to make disagreeable faces at each other and pick quarrels, so we were very glad to see the last keg unloaded and the gang plank pulled on board the boat (her name was *Scorpion*) and her mooring cast free.

Then the ponies moved off, with the Land-Rover just ahead of them. As we mounted and prepared to follow the minibus, I realised that dusk had fallen and Pennecford's half-dozen street lamps were lit. We splashed along through the high tide back to the Baybourne road. We didn't take any of our usual paths up Menacoell because there is one on the south-east corner which starts much nearer Pennecford and, with careful driving, you can get a Land-Rover three-quarters of the way to the cottage, a fact which Image Films seemed to know. They left the minibus on the road, Marty and the blonde got in the Land-Rover and various spotlights and floodlights were switched on to light up the scene.

It was slow going for despite their 'acclimatisation period' the smugglers didn't seem very fit and they had to take frequent rests, but at least our ponies were less irritable over delays for we simply let them graze until the cavalcade moved on again. For the last bit, when the Land-Rover had to be abandoned, everyone seemed to be wandering round with handheld cameras and portable lights and the unloading scene outside the cottage looked a muddle with loose ponies milling round and the smugglers colliding as they hurried the kegs into the cottage.

Then we were told that the ponies were ours and we struggled to sort out the confusion. Ginge was quite nice and helped us, turning round ponies, handing up reins, but everyone else disappeared: Marty and the camera team down the path to the Land-Rover, taking the portable lights and plunging us in total darkness, and the smugglers into the cottage from which, in a few minutes came the delicious and tantalising smell of frying bacon and eggs.

We got out our torches and gave the best ones to Carolyn and William, who said they would light our way as far as Chilmarth. Louisa took one of Mick's ponies and Strongbow, weary and less apprehensive after an evening surrounded by panniers, seemed willing to lead the other. The first part of the journey down was very difficult with the path too narrow for three ponies abreast, and the slipping and slithering over the rough-going was even more unnerving in the variable light of the torches. I could see exactly what Felix meant about pack ponies always going in single file and I wished we had had time to train ours to go in a long string.

When we reached the road we said goodnight to the Mitchells, rather envying them their quick return to home comforts, while we had a long dark journey ahead. Heather decided that we couldn't risk a journey across Middle Moor with so many of us leading two ponies and only Huw and Tracy to light the way. So we rode back by the road, lamenting the extra miles, but glad of the undemanding going. The few cars which passed us were being driven cautiously by people who knew the hazards of wandering cattle and herds of ponies on the moor roads.

The Jackson ponies were delighted to see Black Tor lane, but Redwing did just suggest for a moment that it would be much better if we left them to go the last part without us and went straight home to Rosebank and supper. However, when my legs told her where her duty lay, she went without argument. Mr. Jackson came out to help us with the panniers. He had decided that all the ponies which couldn't be fitted into the stable were to be turned out in a field that was shut for hay.

'He'll regret it later,' said Heather, slamming the gate shut as the last pony was freed and buried its nose in the short, lush grass.

We rode home with the Hamiltons and Jane. Toby and Jane, who seemed rather dazzled by Marty Coombes, would only speak in his voice and call us Pardner or Sweetie according to sex. Felix grew more and more irritated and suddenly burst out, 'If you ask me his accent's as phoney as everything else in that set up.'

'Oh, rubbish,' said Toby, 'and what do you know about American accents?'

'Not much,' agreed Felix, 'but I've done enough filming at school to know when the lens cap is still on the camera, and it was, all through that unloading scene; they didn't take one solitary shot!'

This was a bit of a bombshell. I began to wonder if Felix could be right, but Toby had an arguing point.

'It could have been just a run-through — a rehearsal for tomorrow. Good cameramen plan their shots.'

'And now more than ever with film the price it is,' Jane backed him up.

Felix sighed and didn't seem to want an argument, so I asked, 'Could it have been a rehearsal?'

'It could but why go through all the motions of filming? Who did he think he was fooling? You don't usually press the trigger when you're just lining up tomorrow's shots.'

Mummy and Daddy greeted us as though we were long-lost children, but when we had settled the ponies and were sitting at the kitchen table ravenously wolfing scrambled eggs, they began to complain. They said that they really didn't like us being out so late and *must* we get mixed up with film companies and wasn't Mr. Jackson just using us all?

We explained that it was highly educational for us to meet all these extraordinary characters and that it *was* only for one more night. Then they began to say that perhaps it was all right for me, but Louisa was too young. Louisa hastily pointed out that if Tracy and Huw were allowed to go by their parents it would be ridiculous to stop her.

Then we began to imitate Marty Coombes for them and to describe Ginge and Kev. We told them how angry Felix was about the fairy lights on the Mariners' Arms and gradually they relaxed and began to take it all less seriously. I didn't dare tell them about Felix's suspicions, much as I would have liked their advice. I could see that the least suggestion that the film wasn't on the level would be the last straw and we would be forbidden to go. And, whatever was going to happen, I wanted to be in on it to the bitter end.

NINE

In the light of next day, Felix's suspicions did seem unlikely and I decided that despite the fact that his father made films about unexplored foothills and his own experience at school he wasn't really an expert and it might well be an instance of a little knowledge being a dangerous thing.

I couldn't see any point in hiring ponies, dressing as smugglers and trailing up and down Menacoell unless you actually did want to make a film of it. But I didn't have all that much time to think about Image Films Ltd, because Mummy dragged us off to Baybourne for a dentist's appointment and after that she said she was ashamed of our jeans and shoes and there was more dragging, this time round the shops. We got home at half-past one and had just started to eat ham and salad — or Louisa and I had, Mummy was on the telephone talking to someone, who went on and on about a Bring and Buy sale — when Toby's face appeared round the back door. He looked pale and worried and he asked straight away, 'Have you seen Felix and Huw?'

We said no and explained about Baybourne.

'No one's seen them,' he told us dramatically. 'I've been to the Jacksons', I've telephoned the Mitchells and Jane is out. They went off quite early, about ten.'

'Didn't they say where they were going?'

He produced a crumpled note from his pocket. I smoothed it out and read, '*Gone to investigate Menacoell. Felix.*'

Suddenly all my earlier misgivings about the men came back. My spine seemed to prick and tingle with suspicion. I felt like a bristling dog.

'Ten, eleven, twelve, one, two,' said Louisa, counting on her fingers. 'They've hardly had time to get there and back yet.'

'But supposing he's right, supposing they are a gang of crooks?' Toby looked so worried. I asked, 'Why didn't you go too?'

'We had a row. He would keep saying Marty Coombes was a phoney. But supposing he is? My mother's gone off miles somewhere about some special tiles Dad says we've got to have for the kitchen floor. She'll be in an awful state when she comes back and finds that Huw's missing.'

Louisa and I looked at each other and sighed. 'Have you brought Patchy?' I asked.

'No, only the bike.'

'Well, go and fetch him. We'll ride over Middle Moor with you and I expect we'll meet them coming back.'

Toby looked relieved. 'Back in ten minutes,' he said.

'And eat some lunch,' Louisa called after him. 'You can't search on an empty stomach.'

I felt angry with Felix. Why did he have to go and vanish? I didn't want to wear Redwing out looking for him when she was already doing the filming; I wondered what a gang of crooks would do to boys who came nosing round.

Mummy came back and collapsed into her chair. 'Oh hell, what a *nuisance*! Mrs. Redstone has let Sheila Sinclair down over the Bring and Buy. I've got to go over and help her price everything for tomorrow. Will you two be all right? There's cake for tea in the tin and I shall insist that I've got to be back by six.'

The meal ended in a rush, as meals always seem to in our house, and Mummy departed in her car just as Toby came down the drive on Patchy.

All the way across Middle Moor I hoped against hope that I would suddenly catch sight of Felix and Huw. Toby said they were still wearing their khaki parkas so with a brown and a dun pony we weren't likely to spot them very far off. I wished desperately that they would reappear, with Felix admitting grudgingly that Marty Coombes was after all on the level. Part of my desperation was because I had absolutely no idea what to do if Felix didn't turn up. The police had checked and said the film company was all above board. The pricking of my spine, now joined by sinking feelings in my stomach, was not the sort of evidence to convince them that London could be wrong.

We didn't spread out and search because it was unlikely that two people would both be lying with broken legs in the heather, and secretly we all felt that if there was any disaster it would be at the cottage. Louisa kept looking at her watch and I knew that she was thinking that every minute which passed, without the boys coming in sight, made it more likely that something really had gone wrong.

When the path branched left and we headed for Menacoell, our eyes searched its rugged height for any sign or movement. As we came to the road we wondered doubtfully which path they would have taken for we had shown Felix three different ways up to the cottage. We stood on the road and shouted, 'Felix, Huw,' several times, but there was no answer.

Then, as we weren't a strong enough party to divide, we chose the first and left-hand path as the one they were most likely to have taken, and began the long climb despondently, not daring to discuss what we were going to do when we reached the terrace. We had climbed for about ten minutes, hardly exchanging a word for we were all engrossed in dismal and nerve-racking thoughts, when suddenly Patchy stopped, raised his head, sniffed the air and neighed. We all stopped and listened and thought we heard an answering neigh farther on the left, over towards Lanvet. Patchy neighed again. We looked for a path going that way and then we rode on shouting, 'Felix, Huw!' We let Patchy lead because our ponies didn't seem very interested. Redwing would have been if she thought it was a lost foal as she has lots of maternal instinct. Then Toby shouted again and this time we were certain that we heard an answer. Our spirits rose and we cantered along the path. Even if something had happened — Huw had fallen off or Minstrel had gone lame — it would be a small thing in comparison with our fears. We came to the edge of the Croft Lanvet fields and there out on the moor beyond, coming along by the stream, was Huw, leading Bellboy, and behind, following loose, was Minstrel.

We waved and shouted and looked at each other in amazement. Then the sinking feelings of my stomach trebled. Something serious must have happened. We didn't stop to wonder. With one accord we turned for a run and jumped the wall in front of us. We galloped, cutting across the fields, jumped two or three more walls, and came to Huw. He looked frightened and exhausted and his face was all streaked and blotched with tears.

'They've got Felix and Jane,' he sobbed as soon as we reached him. 'The smugglers have got them. Felix told me to gallop, so I did and their ponies followed.'

We gradually got the story out of him. Felix had said he must know if there was anything in the kegs. He'd quarrelled with Toby so he asked Huw to go with him as pony holder. He had called at our house, but we were at the dentist's, and then he'd collected Jane. They'd ridden up Menacoell and found the cottage deserted. Felix had stationed Huw and the ponies on the hillside at the back of the cottage behind the outhouse wall and then he and Jane had gone to investigate. Bored, Huw had moved along the wall to a building which had fallen down and there, by sitting on Minstrel, he could see over. Felix and Jane had gone right into the cottage and been there several minutes when he heard voices. He thought the smugglers must have gone in at the front door, just as Felix and Jane crept out of the back, and began to run for the ponies. There had been angry shouts and running feet and Jane was overpowered quite quickly, but Felix managed to make the wall. He'd said, 'Take this and gallop,' and flung a packet over. Then he'd run along the wall towards a place low enough to climb and three smugglers caught up with him and pulled him down. Huw hadn't waited to see what had happened after that.

'And what was it he threw?' I asked. 'Have you got it?'

'Yes.' Huw fished in his pockets and produced a packet of thick, transparent plastic containing a white powder. Louisa and I looked at each other and then suddenly all my indecision vanished. I knew exactly what to do. 'If you and Toby can lead the two ponies home, I'll gallop ahead,' I said, taking the packet.

'Once Daddy's got this analysed it'll be proof.'

'But we can't just leave Felix,' protested Toby, but even as he said the words he seemed to recognise their uselessness, and as I started downhill I heard Louisa saying, 'They'd just catch us too and then no one would know *where* to look.'

Redwing and I both enjoy cantering downhill, so with the stolen packet zipped securely in my anorak pocket, we cantered whenever the path made it possible and quickly reached the road. Across Middle Moor she simply flew, seeming to sense that we had an urgent mission. Three times I made her walk for a breather because she is one of those generous ponies who would let you gallop them to death without the smallest complaint. I kept my mind off Felix and Jane and what *might* be happening to them and concentrated on reaching the Health Centre in one piece; it wasn't until I came to St. Dinas and slowed up for a fourth breather, that I let myself think at all. Once we knew what the powder was people would listen to us — unless it turned out to be something quite ordinary like cornflour. I almost laughed as I thought of this. But if it were, if Felix's suspicions and my misgivings were wrong, why had the smugglers set upon Jane and Felix? They might have thought they were intruders, stealing sleeping bags and dirty socks. And if they had? Well, they would either set them free or take them to the police station, and everyone would agree that we had a perfect right to the cottage.

I cantered along the last bit of the grass verge, saw Redwing's longing look at Rosebank, and dropped down into the world of narrow roads between high banks, where a trot is the best you can do. We trotted past the Penhydrock gate, into Ruveland and across the Health Centre car park. I flung myself off, opened the door and called, 'Miss Gurney!' loudly and urgently. Surgery wasn't until six; I knew that Mrs. Cole wouldn't be there, but Miss Gurney should be minding the telephone, typing letters full of symptoms to consultants, filling in forms ... 'Miss Gurney!' I yelled.

She came at last, white-overalled and shocked that the orderly calm of the surgery should be broken by my yells.

'Whatever on earth is the matter?' she demanded.

'Something serious, I need Daddy.' I produced the packet. 'We have to get this powder analysed at once.'

'That's a tall order. Your father's at the hospital and he has several quite urgent calls to make afterwards. I don't expect him back till six.'

'Can't you get him?'

'I expect he'll ring by and by to see if there are any emergencies.'

'What about Dr. Grant?'

'He'll be back at six for surgery.'

I felt despondent. All that speed for nothing. 'It really is important,' I told her. 'Well, I'd better write Daddy a note. Will you hold Redwing a minute please?'

I wrote quite a long note explaining everything. About Jane and Felix and how we thought the powder was from the kegs and how we would be unloading the second shipment at high tide. I put the note and the powder together and then I wrote TERRIBLY URGENT. MATTER OF LIFE AND DEATH! on another sheet of paper-clipped it on top of them and arranged them all prominently in the centre of Daddy's desk.

'What a dear, gentle creature,' said Miss Gurney patting Redwing nervously.

'You will tell him? It really is terribly urgent,' I said as I mounted. I rode slowly. Redwing seemed a bit tired now that the excitement was over. I wished that she didn't have to go out again. I patted her, told her she was almost a heroine and promised her a rest next day. It wasn't time for the Jacksons yet so I watered Redwing, gave her a small feed and then went indoors to feed myself. Soon I heard hoofs and Louisa rode in. She said she'd turned Bellboy out in his field and Toby and Huw had gone home; had I found Daddy? Her face fell when I answered no and explained about my message. 'We'll have to go through with tonight then?'

'Unless they put it off.' We watered and fed Spider and then we ate all we could and stuffed our pockets with useful food and found the torches.

We set off for Black Tor Farm in good time and Toby overtook us on the way.

'Mummy wasn't there,' he said. 'She'd been back

and left a note asking where we all were giving a telephone number of the place where she was going next. I
rang the number, but she hadn't got there yet, so I left
a message that Huw was all alone. I got some tea and
made him promise not to do anything silly. He's not as
young as all that and he's got Casper our Collie to
protect him.'

'Our mother's not at home either,' said Louisa,
'otherwise she would have taken him in. And Daddy
wasn't to be found, worst luck, but Frances has left
messages and a note and the powder, so we'll just
have to hope.'

'I don't think they'll turn up, the smugglers, I mean,'
observed Toby. 'If they recognised Jane and Felix, and
they caught Jane once before, they will do a bunk
surely?'

'But if they didn't see Huw they may think we
don't know what has happened to the others. After all,
if the ponies had come home with empty saddles we'd
have to search the whole moor. It could take days. No,
I think they'll come if they're on the level,' I continued,
'or, if the cargo's *really* valuable, it may be worth
taking a risk.'

'I'd land it on some dark little beach at dead of
night,' said Toby.

'But those are the places where the coastguards keep
watch,' I told him, 'for illegal immigrants as well as
smuggling.'

'They'd have to be very small immigrants to fit in
those kegs,' said Toby with a nervous giggle.

At Black Tor all was in ferment. Marty Coombes
had telephoned and asked for the ponies an hour earlier

and Mr. Jackson had said he would do his best. Heather said it wasn't his best, but ours, and half-an-hour was the most he could hope for. Despair deepened when we said that Felix and Jane wouldn't be coming and then they were all absolutely horrified when we told them what had happened.

'Oh,' said Heather, 'that explains something else Marty Coombes told Dad. He'd heard there were two children lost on the moor, and asked if we'd been looking for them. Dad said, "They're not our children, we've got all ours, must be visitors from London." I heard him say it. Poor Dad, he always gets everything wrong.'

'It's the best thing he could have done as far as we're concerned, he may have put them off their guard.'

We had a difficult time sorting out a way of taking the extra ponies. Louisa could take two, but Tracy couldn't lead anything from Dickon. In the end we solved it by putting Poppy's panniers on Misty and then Tracy rode Poppy and led Misty with two sets and Dickon without any. Then, cursing panniers and all hoping we'd never see any again after that night, we set off to meet the smugglers.

TEN

They were all waiting in the Lanvet lane and Marty Coombes snapped that we were late and hardly gave us time to get the saddle off and the panniers on Poppy, before he had the smugglers marching up the road at a brisk pace.

'Now, I don't want you kids crowding us tonight. We're going to record some sound effects and we don't want your voices on the track. So keep back, right back; understand?'

We understood all too well, or we thought we did. He was up to something and didn't want us to see. But Heather put on her trekking-centre voice and promised to keep well back.

'It would be better still if you took yourselves off for two to three hours and met us back here at half-nine. We should be through by then.'

We looked at each other in dismay, but Heather was ready for him. 'Dad wouldn't like that at all,' she answered. 'He said we were to stay around in case you had trouble with any of the ponies. If we go home I expect he'll be out to keep an eye on things in the

Land-Rover.' The mention of Mr. Jackson implied a slight threat and Marty Coombes recognised it at once.

'O.K. then, but remember what I said.'

'He's losing his accent,' said Toby gloomily as the minibus drove off in pursuit of the smugglers.

'We could go up to Menacoell now and set Felix and Jane free,' suggested Mick.

'They'll have left a guard,' said Toby.

'If they are still up there. My guess is that they're gagged and bound and inside that,' I said, as the dark blue props van passed us and joined the procession. We rode in grim silence for a bit and then Heather said, 'I think if he's so anxious to get rid of us we'd better stick to him like burrs.'

'Yes, and another hour or two at Menacoell won't really hurt them. But supposing he tried to put them on the boat, we'd have to be ready to put a stop to that,' said Louisa.

'I suppose we could get people from the pub to help us.' Toby was looking pale and desperate.

'Weren't many there last night,' said Mick gloomily.

As we passed Chilmarth, William and Carolyn came out to join us, they were horrified at the thought of Felix and Jane being held prisoner, and wanted to go straight home and telephone the police. But Mick, Heather and I felt it would be senseless to have the police before at least some of the cargo was unloaded; Marty would simply signal to the boat to go away and get on with his filming and everyone would tell us we were imagining things. In the end we agreed on a plan. As soon as the kegs were in the panniers, some of us

would trot up Ship Street and dial 999 from the telephone box outside the post office and tell the police
that we had reason to believe that the kegs contained
an illegal cargo. And, if it turned out that we'd made
fools of ourselves, well, that was just too bad.

I think we all felt a lot happier once we had a
sensible plan and then, as the pack ponies all seemed to
be behaving perfectly, we all decided to cut across the
fields, reach Pennecford before the smugglers, and so
get a good position where we could see exactly what
was going on and off the boat.

We came down the lane and rejoined the Pennecford
road at St. Nechtan; we noticed that there was a telephone box on the corner below the church. Then we
rode on, splashing through the full tide to Pennecford
where we checked that there was still a telephone box
in Ship Street. At the quay we dismounted to give our
weary steeds a rest, and took up the same position as
we had the evening before. There was only one boat
coming up the estuary and William produced his father's
binoculars and announced that it was *Scorpion* and she
still had her fancy rigging. I was looking at the row of
fairy lights along the Mariner's Arms and hoping that
nothing awful had happened to Felix and Jane. Kidnap-
pers who panic sometimes kill their victims. I didn't
think Ginge would, but Marty Coombes? I wouldn't
put it past him; he was charming enough, but it was
the sort of charm that turned on and off like a tap. We
must keep close watch on *Scorpion*. Supposing after
they had unloaded the kegs and sent the ponies on their
way, they backed the blue van up to the quay and
brought out two large packing cases? Well-weighted

people sank without trace at sea. It was a horrible thought. It didn't bear thinking about. I looked at my watch: seven-fifteen. Unless Daddy had had a really bad emergency or accident he must have read my note . . .

Our ponies' heads went up suddenly and we heard the steady clip-clop of approaching hoofs. It would make a nice sound-track, I thought, if they were really recording. But had hard roads been in existence in the days of smuggling? I felt sure that if Felix had been there he would have said Macadam wasn't born or, if he was, it was much too soon for this sort of road to exist in country districts; hoofs would have squelched through mud, or scrunched on stones, not clipped and clopped.

Scorpion had been watching for the ponies and as they arrived she changed course and began to come in. Marty Coombes jumped out of the minibus and gave us a very dirty look − I suppose he was wondering how we came to be there first − before he addressed *Scorpion* through the loudhailer. As her crew went through the rigmarole of lowering the false bulwark, Marty turned to speak to the smugglers. 'Now, pardners, we want a bit more action. Remember we've just gotten a message that the Excisemen are on their way; make it lively.'

They did. The whole scene became a terrible muddle. No sooner had the boat touched the quay than the gang plank was down and the smugglers aboard. They rushed backwards and forwards carrying kegs anyhow and colliding with each other. The ponies had mostly been left unattended: Gipsy and Mousie had organised a mutual scratching session, Trudy had gone to sleep and Mick had to sprint through the middle of everything to grab Crackers, who was just setting off for home. I expected a shout of fury from the cameraman, but nothing happened.

Heather was still trying to point out to Kev that he'd put more kegs in one pannier than the other, giving Pirate a hopelessly unbalanced load, when the cavalcade set off at a jog trot. I looked round for the blue van, it was already moving after the ponies, and *Scorpion* had her false bulwark aboard and was already turning away from the quay.

'You keep back! Wait there till we've reached the corner. I don't want you messing things up!' Marty Coombes sounded quite vicious, so we gave him a short start before we moved forward to the bottom of Ship Street. William and Carolyn, who had volunteered to be telephoners, trotted up it and the rest of us slunk slowly after the smugglers wishing for hoof-pads or a grass verge.

Then the Mitchells came clattering incautiously after us. Their faces told us something was wrong. 'The box has been ripped to bits. There's a notice saying it's been 'vandalised' and will be repaired as soon as possible,' said William. 'We'll have to use the St. Nechtan one.'

'Couldn't you have used the post office's private one?'

'It was shut and think of the explanations. The St. Nechtan one will do just as well.'

I didn't want to wait a minute now that the kegs were in the panniers. I didn't like Marty Coombes's changed face or the speed with which the smugglers were vanishing up the road. We *had* to follow them and what would Marty do when he found we had disobeyed his instructions? It was dusk now and I could see St. Nechtan's solitary street lamp and its circle of light mirrored in the wet road.

Then suddenly the clop of hoofs stopped. The minibus pulled into the side, the big van swung across the road and then backed into the lane beside the church. It backed slowly, and as our view of the road became clear again we saw that it was empty. Both smugglers and ponies had vanished.

We broke into a trot and then walked again as we came up to the van. It filled the lane, but through the narrow gap between it and the church wall we could see the ponies, lit up by the Land-Rover's lights, and the smugglers grabbing the kegs from the panniers and bundling them into the van. And as they finished with each pony they gave it a thump and bundled *it* through the gate into the churchyard.

William had dismounted and made for the telephone box. It seemed terribly foolhardy to be dialling 999 right under the noses of the smugglers and he stood there in the box, lit for all the world to see, and obviously one of us in his crash cap.

Then Louisa gave a cry of horror: 'The ponies will eat yew!' It was true. We all realised instantly that there were several yew trees in the tiny churchyard and hungry ponies might easily snatch a mouthful of the first greenery they found in the dark. The lane was out of the question, but there was an alleyway between the cottages and some steps went up to a lych gate. We could get into the churchyard that way and catch the ponies as the smugglers turned them loose. The cottages were built up above the road to be out of the high tide and in front of them ran a narrow walkway with an iron rail. With one accord we tied our ponies to the rail and then, except for Mick who said, 'I'll hang on for William,' we rushed up the steps and into the dark churchyard. The ponies were stumbling about between the graves. I left Misty, who was tearing ravenously at some long grass round a neglected tomb, and went to collect Crackers who was standing by a yew and watching the activity in the lane. The smugglers had almost finished their unloading. They were going to get away! I just hoped that Jane and Felix weren't in the blue van. I got Crackers, plus his panniers, through the lych gate and then he went down the steps in a series of flying leaps and towed me into the road where we almost collided with a black police car slinking silently to a halt at the sight of the ponies and the minibus.

'Where are they?'

'Up the lane there, loading the kegs into the van. You can get through the churchyard,' I pointed, 'but there are about ten of them.' Then I saw that there was another police car behind and another and another and soon the road was jammed and the whole place full of hurrying police. Then there were shouts and running feet and the sounds of blows and scuffles. And as we all ran back to the churchyard to collect more ponies, we heard the sound of the minibus starting up. It couldn't get out for there were police cars right across the road, and as I came to the steps with Silver Sand I saw it reversing wildly down the road to Pennecford. The smugglers knew as well as we did that the road ended there, but they could take a boat and get away by sea. Then I saw a police car going in pursuit and, as I tied Silver Sand to the railing, I heard a loud crash as though someone had reversed very hard into a wall.

We were searching for ponies in the churchyard when the fighting ended and the police switched on lights: car lights and torches, portable lights brought out of the boots of police cars, the film company's lights, a light in the lych gate, a light in the church porch. We retrieved Pirate and Poppy, from what had been a very dark corner, and went down to count the ponies. They were all there but Drummer and we could hear him neighing mournfully from the lane. Mick ran to fetch him and the rest of us tried to deal with a police sergeant who wanted to know how many smugglers they ought to have caught. We counted up: Marty and the blonde, the six from Menacoell, the cameraman and three drivers. We described Marty Coombes carefully, but we didn't say anything about Ginge. I quite hoped he'd got away.

It was Toby who remembered Felix and Jane. 'My brother and a girl called Jane Shaw,' he was telling the sergeant. 'We think they're locked up somewhere at Menacoell, but they might be in that van. Could you start looking for them as soon as possible?'

The sergeant turned to a constable. 'Find out if 101's here yet. They should have everything under control,' he told Toby. 'We sent them out the moment we heard from Dr. Burnett.' Then he went off to count his prisoners, who were all being bundled into a Black

Maria. The constable said, 'Hang on a minute,' and going to the nearest car he began to speak on the radio. 'They've got them,' he called to us. 'They should be here somewhere. I daresay they're keeping them in the car till they're sure the fracas is over. Hang on while I see.'

When he came back he had Mummy and Daddy and P.C. Weston as well as Felix and Jane. And two seconds later Mr. Jackson, Mrs. Hamilton and Huw appeared. Everyone talked at once. Felix and Jane seemed all right, but a bit dazed.

Jane said, 'It was awful, they nailed us up in a dark sort of pigsty place. We couldn't stand up straight and all we had to eat was some bread Ginge threw in to us.'

'It would have been much worse if Huw hadn't got away; at least we knew he was sure to get help eventually,' added Felix, 'and thank goodness you knew what to do with the powder.'

Daddy, who had been talking to P.C. Weston, said, 'Yes, I had a fairly good idea what it was and being a medical man the police took me seriously ...'

'They'd have taken you seriously anyway,' P.C. Weston told him. 'We knew there was a gang operating. We'd heard there was a consignment expected. That 'Mr. Carter' your daughters found is a member of the drug squad, come down from London to give Baybourne a hand. He'd had a tip-off that they'd found a stately home as a base and, doing the rounds, he came upon this couple of lads at Tolkenny, started asking questions and got beaten up. I suppose they panicked. Then they must have found Menacoell, thought no one went near it for one year to the next, and it was very handy for the estuary.'

'And that amount of heroin is worth a fortune,' said Daddy, 'a large fortune; they could afford to go to a bit of trouble setting up this film company front.'

Mummy, who had been talking to Louisa, suddenly came over and gave me a smacking kiss. Then she looked at the long row of ponies and said, 'How on earth are you going to get that lot home?'

'There's only twenty there,' I said. 'Yesterday we had twenty-three. We'll ride and lead them.'

'But it's pitch dark,' Mummy objected.

The police seemed to be laying claim to the panniers and pack saddles, so we helped Mr. Jackson and Mick who were taking them off and never have I been so glad to see the back of anything: I disliked the panniers almost as much as Marty Coombes.

Felix and Jane said they were going to ride home with us. They could easily manage bareback on Trudy and Misty. Huw said he was coming too and that sparked off an argument with his mother. Daddy said he couldn't because he hadn't got a crash cap, but Huw said he had, he'd brought it just in case, and ran off to collect it from his mother's car. Louisa said he could have Spider who was complete with saddle and she would ride Poppy bareback, if Tracy wanted Dickon and the saddle. Then the Mitchells decided they would come with us and lead a pony apiece. That meant eleven riders to nine led ponies and Heather said with Huw and Tracy to light the way and only one led pony each we could go over the moor. The mothers began to object again but Mr. Jackson swamped them with optimistic statements.

'Know the moor like the back of their hands. Couldn't have a quieter lot of ponies. Children can see in the dark.'

William was organising Daddy. 'If you'd just call in on our parents, tell them what's happened and ask my father to come and collect us from the Jacksons' in the horse-box. Carolyn and I won't want to hack all the way back.'

P.C. Weston lent me his torch that clipped on a belt and left your hands free and Felix lent me his belt to wear over my anorak. At last we sorted out who was to lead what, and mounted. The police had driven the blue van out of the lane so we rode past the church and into the Chilmarth fields.

We all felt hungry but cheerful. Felix gave cries of anguish at intervals because he said Trudy's immense breadth was doing terrible things to his legs, but he wouldn't swop with anyone, so I don't think it was as bad as he made out.

Louisa was worried about the smugglers having to spend years and years in prison and wondered if it was their own faults or if they had been affected by horrid childhoods. William told her very firmly that they were just in it for the money, easy money, and of course it was tempting when you could make a year's income in a couple of days. And Carolyn said, what about the people who took heroin and got hooked on it and died? That was much worse than prison.

I was thinking about Menacoell, how it was ours

again and we could camp there in the summer, all of us, if Jane and Felix hadn't been put off it for life.

Then we came up on the moor and Redwing, walking briskly, pricked her ears and sniffed the wind-stirred dark. The moon was small, waning, Mick said, not new, and Felix and Toby were actually agreeing on which stars were the plough. Huw came to ride with me because he said Spider wanted to be with Redwing, and asked if I knew that this was only the second time he had ever ridden in the dark?

'Life's quite different down here,' he told me. 'Dad said it would be, but I didn't really believe him. We've *never* had so many adventures in a week before and in the Home Counties no one *dreams* of going for rides at night.'

'It's having the moor,' I said. 'Wild places make things happen. And ponies which are bred on moors are used to finding their way by moonlight and starlight and even in the dark.'

'Yes, and now we've become star-riders too. Not show-jumpers or eventers but star-riders of the moor.'